THE BEAT

Dead White Male

Everybody's got something to hide.

The blackmailer hangs around opposite the Park-and-Ride scheme of a Saturday morning. He does a lot of hanging around, watching. You never know what you'll see.

On Radford Road, the blackmailer passes a police officer. The officer pauses, only half-recognizing him. The blackmailer smiles, then walks quickly on… For police officers, too, have secret lives. They have things to hide. And people who have things to hide will pay to keep them quiet…

Other titles by David Belbin in the Point Crime series:

Avenging Angel
Break Point
Deadly Inheritance
Final Cut
Shoot the Teacher
The Beat: Missing Person
The Beat: Black and Blue
The Beat: Smokescreen
The Beat: Asking For It

Coming soon in Point Crime:

Bored to Death
Margaret Bingley

Lawless and Tilley: The Secrets of the Dead
Malcolm Rose

Fade to Black
Stan Nicholls

POINT CRiME

THE BEAT

Dead White Male

David Belbin

SCHOLASTIC

Scholastic Children's Books
Commonwealth House, 1–19 New Oxford Street,
London WC1A 1NU, UK
a division of Scholastic Ltd
London ~ New York ~ Toronto ~ Sydney ~ Auckland

First published in the UK by Scholastic Ltd, 1996

Copyright © David Belbin, 1996

ISBN 0 590 13898 7

Typeset by TW Typesetting, Midsomer Norton, Avon

Printed by Cox & Wyman Ltd, Reading, Berks.

10 9 8 7 6 5 4 3 2 1

PROLOGUE

Everybody's got something to hide.

The blackmailer hangs around the Park-and-Ride scheme on the Forest of a Saturday morning. He does a lot of hanging around, watching. You never know what you'll see. That woman, for instance, driving in with her husband from leafy Wollaton, big bump in her stomach. If her husband knew the things she'd got up to when she was fifteen, he'd be off like a rocket.

That student, walking along Gregory Boulevard, has just made a buy. There's a silver-foil wrap concealed in the lining of his leather jacket. True, drugs are everywhere. But he's a medical student. If he got caught carrying, they'd never let him become a doctor.

There are two police officers walking down Mount Hooton, doing their beat. The blackmailer, not wanting to be noticed, turns on to Bentinck Road, as though he was only pausing to tie a shoelace, and walks briskly into Hyson Green.

On Radford Road, outside one of the second-hand furniture stores, the blackmailer passes another police officer. The officer pauses, only half-recognizing him. The blackmailer smiles, then walks quickly on, before the officer can put a name to a face.

For police officers, too, have secret lives. They have things to hide. And people who have things to hide will pay to keep them quiet. The blackmailer was meaning to go home, but heads instead to the Cricketers' for a celebratory pint.

He's just found another victim.

1

Clare's feet hurt. She'd been pounding the beat for eight hours with barely a break. Now she wanted to go home. She wanted to soak in a hot bath with plenty of bubbles for a good hour at least. But Paul Grace, her inspector, "wanted a word" and he hadn't shown up in the station yet.

"How's Henry?" Clare asked her sergeant, Jan Hunt, who was rushing off to pick up her son from the childminder's.

"Teething. See you tomorrow."

As Jan hurried out, a voice chirped from behind a typewriter.

"I don't know how she does it."

Clare was alone in the parade room with Gary, the shift's newest recruit, a chubby-faced, red-haired ex-butcher from Worksop. Clare nearly made a sharp reply: "Same as all the other working mothers in the world," something like that. But Clare didn't know if Gary would take backchat personally. She already had a reputation as the shift's feminist and didn't want to add to it.

"Waiting for someone?" Gary asked, finishing his paperwork.

"Grace. I was supposed to meet him at two."

"The inspector was called over to Bridgford half an hour ago. I wouldn't be sure he's coming back."

Clare swore.

"You in some kind of bother?" Gary asked, concern in his voice.

"Not as far as I know."

"Well, then."

Clare found herself leaving the station with Gary. The two of them walked into the city in the hottest part of the early July day.

"Maybe he only wanted to ask you out tonight," Gary suggested, as they turned into the Market Square. "It is Saturday."

"I don't date policemen," Clare said, making it clear just in case Gary had any ideas along that road. "Anyway, people reckon that Grace is gay."

"On what grounds?"

Clare thought for a moment. This was the police force. People didn't need to justify their prejudices.

"For a copper, he dresses too well when he's out

of uniform: expensive, designer stuff. And he hasn't got a girlfriend anyone knows about. Not that I'm bothered. What he does in his private life is his own concern."

"I'm with you there," Gary said. "It takes all sorts…" Clare reached her bus stop on Queen Street.

"Have you got far to go?" she asked Gary.

"Just up the hill. I'm staying at the YMCA until I find a place." Clare was surprised. She'd always thought the YMCA was for foreign students, transients of one kind or another.

"What's it like?" she asked.

"All right. A roof over my head. It'll do until I suss the city out a bit more. Most places for rent want you to stay six months, minimum. That's a long time to be stuck in an area if it turns out to be a dump."

"I see what you mean."

Clare got on the bus. Guiltily, she watched Gary cross the road, heading for his temporary home. There was a room to rent in her house, had been for several weeks, since Steve moved out. She should have mentioned it. But she didn't want to share rooms with yet another officer, especially not one on the same shift as her. Ruth, Clare's best friend, was also on the job. They'd lived in the same house since finishing their training course at Ryton earlier in the year.

Lately, Clare had been getting lonely. The other women in the house had boyfriends. Ruth had Ben, also a copper on Clare's shift, and spent a lot of time at his flat in Mapperley Park. Sam, their landlady, had recently started going out with her ex-lodger, Steve, for the second time. Steve was an unemployed ex-student with a criminal record, several years Sam's junior. Sam said that she was helping Steve to "mend his ways". All of which left Clare alone in the house more often than she'd like.

She got in at two-thirty. There was no hot water. Ruth must have had a bath just before starting her afternoon shift. Clare switched on the immersion heater, then flopped on her bed. Why did her life seem so sour and meaningless? Not for the first time, she thought about the university career she'd given up a year before, wondered whether leaving had been a mistake. Neil, her ex-boyfriend, had warned her how boring police work could be. She'd thought he was exaggerating.

Clare missed Neil. He'd wanted to marry her; yet, within days of being turned down, he'd got a new girlfriend. He and Clare had promised to stay friends, but things never worked out that way, not after other people showed up on the scene.

At least she and Ruth were going out tonight. Ben had something on with his parents in Mansfield, so Clare and Ruth were supposed to be meeting in the Peacock just after ten, then going to a club, if Ruth's tired legs were up to it. Hopefully, Ruth's sergeant wouldn't have her out walking this afternoon. For Ruth had no one to walk with. Her partner and mentor, Roy Tate, was on suspension, waiting to find out if he'd be taken to court for grievous bodily harm. No one blamed him for what he'd done: beating up a man who had raped his granddaughter. But there was no evidence against the rapist, while several witnesses had seen what Roy did to him. Whatever happened about the court case, his force career was finished. He'd be lucky to keep his pension.

Clare wished that she had a wider circle of friends outside the job. She ought to work on it. But that was silly. Friendships, by definition, weren't something you worked on. They were something which happened naturally. Or didn't. In which case, maybe there was something wrong with her. Maybe she'd made too many mistakes – leaving behind one set of friends when she went off to university, then losing another set when she dropped out. When had she last called Denise, who worked in the city? Soon it would be too late to pick up the pieces. Let a friendship go cold, and it froze to death. Indifference was far more hurtful than a falling out.

Oh, stop being stupid, Clare! she told herself. *You're only twenty years old. You're allowed to make as many mistakes as you want. That's how you learn.* But the question remained: was the life she was living now all one big mistake?

*   *   *

The blackmailer sat in the appointed place, a café on Greyhound Street – a small alley between Long Row and King Street. Georgina Drew came out of the public toilet which was next to the café and spotted the blackmailer in the corner.

"Watcha, George."

She scowled, not liking him to use the old nickname.

"What were you doing in the car park earlier?" she complained. "Spying on me?"

"Spying, sure. But not on you. Why would I need to do that? Though I was surprised to see you. Didn't think you liked to show your face in that part of town."

"It was Eric. He insisted it was easier to park there. There're always queues in the multistoreys. He hates queuing, Eric does."

That was enough chitchat.

"Got the money?" he asked.

The waitress came over to see what George wanted, but he waved her away. Georgina slid an envelope to him beneath the table.

"It's the last time, Scott. With the baby coming, money's short. I've had to pack in work and Eric's on short time."

"Yeah, sure."

"I mean it, Scott. The last time."

Worry lines curled around her eyes. George was

twenty-two at the most. Right now, she looked nearer forty. *The last time?* She knew as well as he did that there was never a last time, not until one of them was in the grave. So what was the point in pretending?

"I'll leave you alone for a while, I promise."

"Not 'for a while', *for ever*. This is getting beyond a joke."

Scott shrugged. "You know the way it works. You don't want Eric to find out, you pay me every so often. We're not talking big money here, George. Thirty, forty quid – a few days' housekeeping. Tell you what. I'll leave it until after you've had the kid. I can't say better."

George stood up, eyes staring daggers. She hissed at him. "You've had enough, Scott. There's thirty quid in that envelope and that's all you're getting. If you breathe a word to Eric, so much as a hint, you're a dead man. I've got friends from the old days, Scott. Friends who wouldn't think twice about giving you a good kicking. Do you hear what I'm saying? I never want to see your weasel face or hear your whining, slimy voice again."

Scott nearly said something. Something like: *Sure, I might end up in intensive care, but your husband would have left you. I'd get better. Your life would be destroyed when your friends found out.*

But he said nothing, only watched with quiet satisfaction as George waddled out of the café.

Probably pregnancy made women uptight. And the stuff about friends from the old days was a load of cobblers, too. She wouldn't dare keep in touch with the few who were left. In time, she would work out for herself what was in her best interests. George was a soft touch. Scott could run her for years, unless someone less generous than him spilt the beans to her husband.

It could, after all, happen any time: today, tomorrow, next month, next year. Maybe it would be in six years' time. Eric and Georgina would show up for junior's first parents' evening and the head-master would say: *Don't I know you?* Then his face would turn red as he realized that the mother sitting opposite used to be a scrubber, and he was one of her regulars, every Thursday, like clockwork, on the Forest after the staff meeting. And Eric would sense it. That night, when the kid was in bed, he would beat it out of George (Eric looked like the violent type). Then he'd throw her out. Within a week, she'd be back on the game. But older, less market-able now than she was when Scott knew her.

Scott liked making up stories like that: *what would happen if* stories. They were good for scaring people with. He had one prepared for Max, the student, too. As for George, he would leave it a while, then go back for more. And she would keep paying. Other people's secrets: they were like shares, which paid a regular dividend. Scott Travis left a pound coin on the table, an amount which included a ten-pence tip. He walked out into the alley, down to Slab Square, feeling like a successful investor, setting out to spend his profits.

2

Neil Foster wasn't looking forward to tonight. He'd been going out with Melanie Byatt for three weeks now and he was happier than he'd ever been, happier than he'd dreamt of being when he was going out with Clare. Melanie, in contrast to his previous girlfriend, was so relaxed, so giving. He didn't know how he'd stand the summer holidays when she went back to stay with her parents. But that was a week away. Tonight, they were going to an end-of-term meal with her pastoral tutor, Professor Dodd.

He'd tried to take a rain check. Taking partners wasn't obligatory, Melanie admitted. But she could do with his support, she said, and, anyway, she wanted to show Neil off. He was worried about being humiliated. When he was going out with Clare, she was always making him feel stupid, sometimes intentionally, sometimes not. Melanie never did that. Even so, Neil knew nothing about English Literature or Humanities. The only book he'd read this year was about football.

And when they got to the Dodds' place, a cosy-looking detached house in West Bridgford, Neil knew that he'd made a big mistake. The leather jacket was all right, though he was too hot in it, but nobody else was wearing a tie. Melanie and Sophie were wearing dresses. Max Walker, a medical student, and Tim Dodd, the professor, were both wearing open shirts and jeans. Elise, Tim's wife, wore a silk blouse and leggings. Neil was seriously overdressed.

"Kim and Lewis went home to their parents early, so it's just the six of us," Tim Dodd announced. He was a thin, pale-skinned man fast approaching forty. "I'm very glad that you could come along, Neil. Melanie's told me about you."

Neil squirmed. Melanie gave him a glance which told him that the professor was exaggerating. She'd have mentioned that she was going out with a policeman, that was all, and he'd be interested. People in his circles didn't mix much with police officers. Dodd probably knew how Neil came to know Melanie. Neil hoped that the recent events at Wordsworth Hall wouldn't be referred to tonight.

What Dodd didn't know, because the girl wanted it kept quiet, was that Sophie Turner had been one of the student rapist's victims.

"You're in CID, I believe," Dodd commented.

"That's right. I transferred in April."

"Must be fascinating."

Neil smiled obligingly. "It's better than walking a beat and dealing with trivial stuff. Plenty of the work is still very mundane: interviews, surveillance, that kind of thing."

"How do you ... you know, *go*, if you're watching someone for hours on end?" Sophie asked.

"We get someone to cover us," Neil told her. "Pop to a pub or whatever. Anyway, I've got a good bladder. You do hear about some of the older guys using milk bottles. Not sure about the women."

Everyone laughed. It was always a sign of a bad evening, Neil thought, when people started laughing at things which weren't remotely funny. He drank his red wine slowly. Melanie had wanted to come in a taxi but Neil insisted on driving, so that they could make a swift and early getaway. He didn't mind only drinking a little. Too much drink and he made a prat of himself. Neil preferred to stay in complete control.

After Neil's five minutes were up, the students talked about their courses – Melanie and Sophie both did English Literature and were finding it dull. Tim Dodd said he was sure things would get more interesting as the course got nearer to the present day. Then Max spoke dismissively about the medical course. Finally, Elise changed the subject to what the three students would be doing in the long holidays. Max was staying in Nottingham, moving into a shared house. Sophie was going home. Neil waited for Melanie's answer with some trepidation. They'd been avoiding the subject.

"I have to be out of hall by next week," she said, "and my parents are expecting me to stay home for ten weeks. Last year, after A-levels, I worked in a pub. This year..." She looked at Neil and smiled. "I'm not so sure."

"Do you two have somewhere to live next year?" Elise asked.

"I'm getting a flat with my friend Lorraine," Sophie said.

"I'll probably rent a room in a house," Melanie mentioned. "There are a few I want to look at this week."

This was news to Neil, too. There was a spare room in his house. But they had only been going out together for a few weeks. That would be rushing things.

After dessert, the conversation soon petered out. There was a serious risk that Professor Dodd would show them his holiday slides of Tuscany. When Neil trotted out his pre-prepared excuse, about having to be on duty early the next day, Max and Sophie both begged a lift off him.

In the car, Melanie and Sophie talked about the English part of their course.

"Maybe Professor Dodd's right," Sophie said. "The course'll get better when we get past all the boring dead white males we're studying at the moment." Neil flinched. The phrase *dead white male* made him think of the job.

"It's true," Mel said. "We haven't studied a single woman writer so far."

"You want to do my course," Max said, in a mocking tone. "We get to study dead white males and females all the time, fresh from the mortuary." Neither girl thought that this was funny.

So far, it had been a good day. Scott had picked up thirty quid from George and spotted that police officer earlier. Max Walker was icing on the cake. Scott had sold him some dope his first week in Nottingham, when he was still doing a little dealing out of pubs on the Green. Max hadn't been back for more. He'd probably found someone who sold better stuff, but Scott had been insulted. He'd worked out a little scam, just for Max. It wasn't so much blackmail, more drug-dealing with menaces. But it had given Scott ideas. He'd gone back to Max every two or three months since then, just when the stupid student was thinking he'd forgotten him. How could he forget? It was Max who'd got him started.

Max wasn't in his room. The light was out. Maybe he was in the pub. Scott was about to head for the Green, meet up with his man Tricky, when a car pulled up. There was a short-haired bloke in the front who looked vaguely familiar, pretty girl next to him. Max got out of the back seat, accompanied by a close-cropped blonde. He had a girlfriend, did he? That'd make him even more keen to avoid embarrassment. But the car waited while Max and the girl went inside, so Scott had to leave it. He lingered by the wall across the boulevard, watching.

Two minutes later, Scott was ready to give up. That was when Max came back out. He must have seen the girl to her door, but not got anywhere. Now he was going for a drink. Scott trotted after him.

"Max, hi. Fancy a pint?"

Max started like a mouse caught in a trap.

"I, eh…"

"You look a bit frazzled, mate. Need a bit of puff to help you chill out later?"

"No. I've already got some."

Max was speeding, Scott observed – he'd have just popped up to his room for a quick snort. Scott had to walk fast to keep up with him.

"Now, now, we've had these little talks before,

haven't we, Max? You scratch my back, I scratch yours. Or would you like me to scratch the back of that nice blonde piece you were with?"

Max stopped, turned round to face him.

"Have you been spying on me? Leave her out of it."

"What's she going to think if her nice student doctor friend gets thrown out of uni for being a druggie, eh?"

"Shut it!"

Max brought both hands up against Scott's chest and pushed him away. Scott was shocked. Max wasn't the violent type. But wizz would do that to a bloke.

"I'm warning you, Max, don't spoil our little arrangement. I've got something for you here. Twenty quid."

"It's the end of term. I haven't got twenty quid. I've barely got enough for a pint. Now..."

As Max swore at him, Scott decided that his timing was off. Timing was important in these things.

"If you don't leave me alone," Max went on, "I'll report you to the police, I will. I know someone in CID..."

"In your dreams."

Max lashed out at him, fists flailing. Scott was so shocked that he didn't think to fight back. He fell to the ground.

"It's over. Leave me alone or I'll have you, God help me. Leave me alone!"

"What's going on?" a man's voice asked.

Max strode off up the hill, to the Grosvenor. He shouldn't have done that, Scott thought. No, he shouldn't have done that. He'd make him pay.

"Are you all right?"

A woman's voice this time. He'd been rescued by a passing couple, concern in their eyes. The man helped Scott up to his feet.

"I think he was on drugs," Scott said. "Asked me for some money, then when I wouldn't give him any, knocked me over."

"That's terrible," the woman said. "You ought to go to the police."

"It's all right," Scott said. "I don't think I'm badly hurt."

"I'd recognize him again," the woman assured him.

"You're very kind."

"Here." The man scribbled on the back of a receipt. "Our address. If you decide to call the police and need a witness."

"Thanks," Scott said. "That's really good of you."

He noted the address. Posh place just up the road in Mapperley Park. Assured that he could walk unaided, the couple continued on their way home. *Soft gets,* Scott thought; nevertheless he tucked the flimsy scrap of paper into the back pocket of his jeans. You never knew when it might come in useful.

3

Most police work is *reactive*. Detectives respond to crimes and try to catch the perpetrators. Recently, however, senior management had decreed that ten per cent of CID's time should be *proactive*. This didn't mean that CID encouraged villains to commit crimes and then caught them. It meant that, using surveillance and other techniques, CID officers tried to catch criminals in the act of committing a crime.

This week, Neil had drawn the short straw. He and Tracey were trying to track down a group of villains who preyed on old people. In the past, crooks like this were looked down on as the lowest of the low. Then they were known as pariahs, even to other criminals. Now they were called specialists:

the *bogus callers*. These men would charge a small fortune for an imaginary repair, like re-tuning the video or clearing the drains. They would pretend to read a meter or check the wiring, stealing whatever they could find in the house. Some returned to the same place again and again, presenting the befuddled but trusting occupants with bills for goods that they hadn't ordered. Often the victims were too embarrassed or confused even to report the crime to the police.

The clear-up rate for these crimes was abysmal: five per cent, at best. The victims might be the most vulnerable members of society, but they also made bad witnesses. Their memories weren't reliable. The victim whose house they were going to today, Mr Bagley, was in the early stages of Alzheimer's disease. He couldn't be sure how many times he'd been ripped off. A defending brief would make mincemeat of him. So, the only way to put the perpetrators behind bars was to catch them at it.

"We're wasting our time here," Tracey said, as they walked up to Mr Bagley's semi-detached house on the Whitemoor Estate. White paint flaked from its pebbledash walls.

"Someone's got to do it," Neil muttered.

He hadn't worked with Tracey before. She was a few years older than him, with a reputation for coarse humour and candid insults. Maybe you had to be that way when you were the only woman in a

CID squad. Yesterday, before she caught the train home to her parents' town, Melanie teased Neil about working at such close quarters with a woman. Neil didn't think of Tracey that way. She might have a strong, not unattractive face, and a pretty good figure, but she played down her sexuality to the point where it barely existed.

"Who are you?" the old man asked, opening his front door without putting on the chain. "Do I know you?"

"It's all right," Tracey said, showing him her warrant card. "We're the police. You asked us to come. Remember?"

The old man shook his head slowly.

"You'd better come in, anyway. Shall I put the kettle on?"

"Thanks," Neil said.

Even in the hottest part of the year, the house smelt of mildew. Tracey looked at Neil and sighed.

"I hope you like to play cards," she said.

Mount Hooton Road was on the edge of two police patches: West, where Clare Coppola worked, and South, which was Ruth Clarke's ambit. The road, which bordered the Forest and Hyson Green, was a notorious venue for prostitutes. Punters kerb-crawled the winding hill, picking the girl they wanted. Price agreed, the girl would get into the car. After which, more often than not, the pair of them would drive into the Forest itself and do their business there.

But prostitution wasn't the beat coppers' problem. They left that to the Vice squad. Some officers got to know the working girls. Their job was to protect them, after all, and they could be useful sources of information. Most ignored them, especially in the dark, when trade was busiest.

One a.m. Ruth thought of it as Monday night, the last night of her shift, but, technically, it was now Tuesday morning. Ruth recognized the girl working the other side of the road, who was waving, but didn't know her name.

"Leave her be," said Brian, Ruth's temporary partner.

Ruth was tempted to agree. Technically, the other side of the Hooton was in West, not South. But then she picked up two of the girl's words above the traffic noise.

"He's dead!"

Brian hurried across the road, dodging traffic. Ruth called it in. Then, before she could cross the road herself, a police Panda sped up out of the Boulevard, siren blaring, screeching to a halt opposite where Ruth stood. Inside it were Clare and her sergeant, Jan Hunt. Ruth ran across.

"What's going on?" Jan asked her.

"I'm not sure. She claims someone's dead. We only just got here." Brian was standing by the girl.

He rolled his eyes to indicate that she was demented. Clare went up to the prostitute, put an arm around her shoulder.

"It's Tracey Wicks, isn't it? What's wrong, Tracey?"

"Down there. I took a punter. He's…"

"The call on the radio. It said someone was dead."

Tracey nodded.

"Show us," Clare said.

The four of them followed Tracey on to Weston Avenue. It was a quiet cul-de-sac full of surprisingly well-to-do houses. The gardens had rockeries and little fountains. The residents, Ruth knew, frequently complained about the activity of prostitutes. Ruth didn't know what to expect. Best bet, she reckoned, was that the punter who'd been with Tracey had dropped dead of a heart attack.

She was wrong. Just inside the gate of one of the houses, Brian's torch picked out a pool of blood.

"The rest of you stop there," Jan Hunt said. "Scenes of Crime won't want our flat feet messing this place up any more than it has been already." Jan radioed in. She gave her call sign.

"Go ahead."

"White male in a collapsed state, Weston Avenue."

"Ambulance?"

Jan leant in.

"No point. It's One-Oblique-One."

This was the code for a sudden death. Ruth was just able to see what she was describing, a dead white male, maybe twenty years old. A slender-looking boy in cheap clothes, covered in blood. It looked like he'd been battered to death.

Brian guarded the area. While Jan waited for the CID night crime officer, Ruth and Clare got into the car with Tracey Wicks.

"What happened?" Clare leapt straight in.

Tracey seemed to know Clare.

"I took a punter back there," she told her. "It was him spotted the body first. He took one look and scarpered. Then I came out and called you lot."

"Did you touch him?" Clare asked.

"What do you think I am, stupid?"

In the light of the car, it was easy to see that there was no blood on Tracey. Whoever had killed the youth would be covered in the stuff. She was not a suspect.

"Why did you choose that house to take your client to?" Clare went on.

"Oh, I like that," Tracey said. "*Client*. Your lot had the house where I used to work boarded up, didn't you?"

Clare smiled apologetically.

"Hold on," Ruth said, wanting to follow procedure. "Full name?"

"Tracey Wicks."

"Age?"

"Fifteen."

Ruth swore under her breath.

"Address?"

She gave the name of a social services home.

"That's where she's meant to be," Clare commented. "Come on, Tracey, tell us where we can really find you."

Tracey gave them the number of a flat in Denman Gardens, nearby.

"It's my boyfriend's."

Ruth and Clare exchanged glances. By "boyfriend", Tracey meant "pimp".

"And the punter?"

"I don't know his name. A darky. Asian. Lives local. A regular."

"Why did you choose that particular house?" Clare asked again, her voice showing frustration at Ruth's dogmatic, routine questions. Ruth was glad that the two of them didn't actually work together. They'd drive each other crazy. Tracey replied in a tone which implied that, if the officers were any good at their job, they'd already know the answer.

"It's empty, innit? Has been for over a year. Any of the others, you run the risk of having things thrown at you from out of a window. They like to empty their toilets on you. It's not worth the aggro."

There went their best chance of finding a witness.

"I don't suppose you have any idea who the victim is?" Ruth asked.

"Maybe," Tracey said. "But I don't know his name. If he's who I think he is, he lives on the Green, not sure where."

The CID duty officer arrived, closely followed by Paul Grace. Clare and Ruth briefed them, then they took Tracey Wicks off for more questioning. Ruth doubted that there was much more for him to find out tonight, but he had to show willing.

Jan and Clare resumed their patrol. Ruth and Brian had to stick around, keeping people away from Weston Avenue. A CID inspector would be along shortly, followed by Scenes of Crime officers with floodlights. First light was only hours away, and there would be a second search of the area then.

All night, cars slowed down, then, seeing Ruth and Brian, sped off again. Some came round more than once, but they were still disappointed. The girls who worked Mount Hooton Road had finished early that night.

Clare came off shift just before six. It was the shift's last day on nights, and everyone looked dog tired, except for Gary, who was in the kitchen area, washing out dirty mugs. While Jan briefed the incoming sergeant on the night's events, Clare wrote a note about the murder on the bulletin board. She wasn't surprised to see Paul Grace in his office, watching her. It was a while since there'd been a major crime during their shift. Clare remembered she'd been meant to see him, after work, when was it? Saturday – ten days ago. Grace hadn't mentioned it since, so the meeting couldn't have been that important. Or maybe it was. Grace was the youngest inspector in the county. He was a busy man. And he had plenty of palms to oil, if he was going to continue his climb up the greasy pole.

"Big night," Grace said to Jan, joining her in the parade room.

"Nothing we couldn't handle."

"Your first murder?" Grace asked Clare.

Clare nodded, frustrated. It had been her first murder. It had happened on her beat, and she hadn't even seen the body. Jan joined them.

"Tired?" Grace asked.

"I guess I'm ready for my rest days," Clare admitted.

Grace frowned.

"Thing is, CID could do with an extra couple of bodies for the next few hours. I can authorize the overtime, if either of you are interested."

"I've got to get off," Jan said.

"Of course."

"I'm up for it," Clare announced.

She had nothing better to do with her time than sleep, anyhow.

"And I could really use the experience," Gary said, suddenly appearing after his sojourn by the sink.

"Eh…"

Clare could read Grace's mind: Gary had been on the force less than a month. CID wanted someone they could rely on. Gary seemed to get the message, too.

"I wouldn't let you down, sir," he said.

Grace hesitated.

"Very well. I'll drop you two off on my way home. This happened practically next door to you, didn't it, Clare?"

"A few minutes' walk."

Most officers found it funny that Clare chose to live in Forest Fields, one of the more crime-ridden areas of the city. But Clare didn't care what they thought. Grace lived out in the dull suburb of Arnold. Therefore, he couldn't get by without a car, whereas Clare could walk to anywhere in the city centre within twenty minutes.

Grace drove a red Mazda sports model. Gary manoeuvred it so that he got the front passenger seat while Clare had to squash into the cramped back area. She listened as Grace chatted to Gary about how he was finding Nottingham. The inspector, when you got him out of uniform, could sound surprisingly sympathetic. They pulled up at Weston Avenue, a hive of activity in the early morning light. Gary got out. Clare was about to squeeze through the passenger door when Grace spoke.

"Actually, Clare, I've been meaning to have a word with you."

"Sir?"

"I don't know if now's the time, but…"

DI Greasby appeared, leaning into the open door.

"Morning, Paul. Brought me two of your finest, have you?"

"I guess now isn't the time," Grace muttered. "I'll talk to you on Thursday."

That was when Clare's next shift began. As Clare got out, Grace exchanged a few words with Greasby. Clare joined Chris Dylan, who was standing next to Ruth. The sergeant had shaved off his moustache, a change of image which might have something to do with his impending divorce. A clean-shaven face made him look younger, a little older than Grace, maybe – thirty, at most, Clare thought – and less like a policeman.

"I was just having a bet with Ruth here," Dylan said, "that they'd send you along. We always seem to end up working together, don't we?"

"Must be fate," Clare said.

Ruth looked irritated.

"Didn't you fancy the overtime?" Clare asked her.

"It's your patch, isn't it?" Ruth said. "Anyhow,

I've done quite enough standing around for one morning, thank you very much."

"Tell them what to do, would you?" Dylan asked Ruth, before wandering off to talk to one of the officers collecting evidence.

Clare looked around for Gary. He was chatting animatedly to Brian.

"Get rid of onlookers," Ruth said, "but if any working girls come by, ask if they've seen anything. Waste of time, really. They've all got the wind up and are staying home."

"Have CID got anything?"

"Not really. They don't know if the lad got killed where we found him, but no one heard anything, so the odds are it happened elsewhere, then the body was dumped. There's no sign of forced entry in the empty house he was found outside, so where it happened is anyone's guess."

"Not much to go on."

"There is one thing. Word is, they found an item in the victim's jeans." Ruth paused.

"Are you going to tell me?" Clare asked, jokily. "Or do I have to beat it out of you?"

Before Ruth could reply, Gary wandered over, looking pleased with himself.

"Hear what they've got? An address, and a bloke's name. It'd be convenient, wouldn't it – if our victim happened to have the killer's name and address in his back pocket?"

4

Neil came on duty that Tuesday morning to find a murder investigation under way. There were no overnight prisoners for him to interview, so he reported to DI Greasby.

"What are you on today?" Greasby asked.

"Tracey and I are babysitting Mr Bagley, waiting for a visit from those bogus repair men, sir."

"You can't have Tracey today," Greasby said. "I've already sent her out interviewing tarts, see if she can find anyone who knows anything about our victim. Want to go out on your own?"

Neil contemplated the endless hours of waiting for someone who probably wouldn't call. Only Tracey made it bearable. The whole operation was a wild shot in the dark, anyway. To get anywhere with bogus callers you needed national intelligence, video surveillance and a whole team dedicated to the job, not two junior detectives with a couple of weeks to spare.

"I'd rather not, sir," he said, and explained the reasons.

"All right," Greasby told him. "Go with Chris. We could do with a third body if chummy's at home. If we get really lucky, he'll make a run for it." Neil joined Chris Dylan and Keith Jones as they drove to a large house in Mapperley Park.

"What do we know about the victim?" Neil asked Chris.

"We got his name through his fingerprints: Scott Travis, age 19. Address not known. Recent convictions for possession of cannabis, crack cocaine and amphetamines. Suspicion of intent to supply, but not enough evidence for a charge."

"What do you reckon his connection is with this bloke we're going to see?"

"Could be his dealer, I suppose. We'll play it by ear."

They pulled up outside the house, a big old semi on the uphill side of Cyprus Road.

"One of you had better stay in the car," Chris said.

Neil tossed Keith for it, and won. After a long wait, a frowzy-looking woman came to the door.

"Yes?"

Dylan showed his badge.

"Mrs Hayne?"

"No, I'm the cleaner. Mrs Hayne's at work."

"And where would that be?"

"She runs the Safe Sex Centre, in the Lace Market."

Chris and Neil looked at each other, trying not to smile at the irony of this.

"And Mr Hayne, what about him?"

"He's a lecturer, at the old university."

"Which department?"

"English. But he's not there now."

"Where is he?"

"In his study, working. Term's all but over."

"Perhaps you could take us to him."

Roger Hayne's study was a small, crowded room. It had overflowing oak shelves from floor to ceiling on three of its walls, each one strewn with books and periodicals. The fourth wall contained a filthy window and a roll-top desk, opened to reveal more clutter in every crevice.

"No computer?" Dylan asked, after introducing the two of them. "I thought that all academics had computers these days."

"I'm a little old-fashioned," Hayne admitted. "My field is mainly the seventeenth century. Shall we go somewhere more comfortable?"

"No, no. This is fine. We're nice and private here."

Dylan didn't want Hayne to be comfortable, Neil realized. Their presence in this cramped room would pile on the pressure.

"What's this about? One of my students?"

"I don't think that the bloke we're here to discuss was ever what might be described as a student," Dylan told him.

"But there's been some kind of crime?"

"You could say that."

Hayne was prematurely balding and bespectacled, but not that old. He was tall. His complexion was good. Neil would bet that he played sport. He had some muscle on him. Physically, at least, he was capable of battering someone to death. But what could his motive be?

"Are you sure that you don't know what this is about?" Dylan asked.

"No. Not at all."

The sergeant produced a photograph from his pocket. It was taken a year ago, after Scott Travis's one arrest. Young people could change a lot in a year, but it was the only one they had.

"Do you recognize this man?"

Hayne looked at it closely.

"I don't think so. I do see so many people, though."

"Think hard."

"No. I'm certain that he's never been one of my students."

"We never suggested that he was," Neil said.

"I'm sorry. But what, then?"

"Have you had any contact of any kind with the young man in this photograph?"

"Not as far as I know, no."

"In that case," Dylan continued, a note of cynicism creeping into his voice, "perhaps you wouldn't mind telling us what your name and address were doing in his back pocket?"

That evening, Ruth woke at six and she took Clare a cup of tea up at eight. According to Sam, her friend hadn't got in until eleven, just as Sam was going off to do her market research interviews for the day. When Ruth went into her room, Clare was still dead to the world. If Ruth let her sleep on, Clare might not wake until midnight. She'd never get into sync for the afternoon shift she was due to begin in two days' time.

"It's so frustrating," Clare said, as they sat down to a late dinner together, "being in on the beginning of an investigation and not being able to follow it through."

"Why don't you ring up Neil? He's bound to know."

"Oh, sure, and what if his new girlfriend answers the phone?"

"If she does, so what?"

Clare shook her head.

"You know, that's how we got together – me pumping him for information – him thinking I was interested in him for himself. All I really cared about was finding out who killed my brother. I can't use Neil that way again."

"We'll have to hold our curiosity then. Never mind. In a year's time, you'll be able to transfer to CID."

"Do you know how long a year is?" Clare asked, ruefully.

Ruth knew how long it could be. She also wondered how Clare would handle it if she ended up working with Neil again.

"Anyway," she said, moving back to the murder, "there probably isn't that much to this case. One low life killing another, that's my guess."

"Motive?"

"Money, drugs or sex."

Clare laughed.

"That's pretty all-inclusive. You might not care, but I'm still curious. It's my first murder."

"Mine too," Ruth acknowledged. "Can't you think of a good reason to call Neil, pop in for a few minutes?"

Clare considered carefully.

"He's still got my Aimee Mann CD," she said. "Now you mention it, I do have a strong urge to hear that again."

Ruth smiled. Clare went to pick up the phone.

*　*　*

After Clare's phone call, Neil rushed around the house, tidying up, the way he used to when the two of them were going out together. Melanie had been gone for over a week now. He hadn't had much incentive to keep the place spick and span. Ruth Clarke's car pulled up just as Neil finished hoovering. He put on a CD of Aretha Franklin's Greatest Hits before answering the door.

"Are you alone?" Clare asked.

She was dressed casually, in T-shirt and jeans. Her hair was a mess. Even so, he still felt a familiar ache.

"Who else would be here?"

Neil walked over to the small pile of CDs he kept by the hi-fi.

"It's none of my business," Clare replied, testily.

"Term's over," he told her. "Melanie's gone back to her parents."

"Oh."

He handed her the CD.

"I didn't think that you liked this," Neil said. "In fact, I could have sworn you told me I could keep it."

"I do like it," Clare protested. "I like it a lot. The only thing was, it's full of these songs about stupid lovers, messing people about, giving up on romance before they've even got started. I thought you were trying to send me a message. That's why I said I didn't like it."

Neil sat down. She'd caught him out, as usual.

"You're right," he said. "I was trying to send you a message. I was trying too hard. Are you trying to send me a message now, asking for it back?"

"No," Clare said.

They stood in embarrassed silence. Neil wasn't sure why she'd really come, but it seemed like a chance to say something. He opened his mouth before he was sure what words would come out.

"I'm getting over you," Neil said, slowly. "Melanie's really good for me: warm, uncomplicated. Not that I'm being critical, or anything, it's just…"

Clare held up a hand to stop him.

"I'm glad," she said.

"What about you?" he asked. "Are you seeing anyone?"

Clare shook her head.

"You know me," she said. "I'm choosy."

Then she paused, trying to decide whether to tell him something. Her voice was hesitant.

"I'll tell you what, though. Or maybe I shouldn't…"

Neil smiled.

"What? Come on."

"Your boss, Chris Dylan. Either he's like that with everyone, or he keeps coming on to me."

Neil nodded.

"He was always interested in you."

"I'm not interested in him."

"His divorce has nearly come through."

"I'm a Catholic girl. I don't believe in divorce."

"Not the only thing you don't believe in."

It was easy to joke about sex now, now that it was no longer an issue between them. Clare half smiled. Then she got up, CD in hand.

"I'd better be going."

Awkwardly, Neil kissed her on the cheek.

"Take care of yourself."

"You too."

It was really over, Clare told herself, as she drove home. She hadn't totally believed it until just now, when she saw another woman's photograph in a frame above the fireplace. How calm Neil had been, how happy he seemed. Clare parked Ruth's car outside the house and went back inside, feeling stupid for feeling so sad.

"Last orders at the Carlton?" she suggested to Ruth. "Sam said she'd be in there."

"Well?" Ruth asked, as they walked up the street.

"We had a nice chat."

"And?"

"The case? I didn't ask him. It didn't seem right somehow."

"Clare Coppola," Ruth said, as they pushed open the bar door, "I do believe you're growing up."

5

"All right," DI Greasby said at the morning briefing, "this is as far as we've got: dead white male, name of Scott Travis. Unemployed. Previous for possession of controlled substances. Today would have been his twentieth birthday. We don't have much to go on. Hopefully, Forensics will be able to tell us whether he was killed where we found him or whether the body was moved. However, at the moment, our only lead is that he had the name and address of an English lecturer, Roger Hayne, in his back pocket. Hayne denies any knowledge of him. Says he gave his address to a boy he saw being beaten up, Saturday before last, in case he needed a witness, but isn't sure if Travis is the one. We don't even have a current address for Travis. We've been to the place that he was signing on from, a house full of bedsits in New Basford, but it seems that the victim was defrauding the housing benefit. He used to go there to pick up his giro, but no one in the building will admit to knowing him.

"What I need, then, is a lot of asking around. What did Travis do, and who with? Where did he live? Use whatever informants you have. Copies of the victim's photograph have been circulated to all the beat coppers in West and South. I've released it to the papers, too. With any luck, by this afternoon, we'll at least know where he lives ... I mean, lived."

He paused and Neil asked a question.

"Am I in on this, sir? Or do I go back to bogus callers?"

"No, stick with Chris. You might learn something. Tracey, I want you to liaise with Vice and keep talking to the working girls. One of them must have seen something."

Tracey grimaced. It seemed unfair that, because she was a woman, she was always the one who had to question prostitutes.

"I've spoken to loads already, boss. They don't know anything."

"Even so, you might get lucky. Chris, go and see Mrs Hayne. Get her at work. Take Neil with you, if you like. Keith, I want you to do another door-to-door around Weston Avenue. See the people who weren't in first time around, then visit the ones we've already interviewed – see if anyone's remembered anything."

Neil accompanied Dylan to the Safe Sex Centre, a clinic for teenagers tucked away on a side street. Elizabeth Hayne was interviewing someone, so they had to wait. The receptionist ushered them into a side room.

"Nothing personal," she said, "but if some of our clients saw you two in the foyer, they'd take one look and bolt off."

Dylan, in his cheap blue suit, looked the archetypal plain clothes copper, Neil realized. Did he look like one, too? He was in grey jeans and a blue denim jacket. He liked to tell himself that he was just another young bloke about town.

As the two men waited, surrounded by posters about the correct use of condoms, Dylan told Neil a filthy joke, involving an elephant, a flea and an inner tube. Neil laughed too heartily. He remembered what Clare had said last night about Dylan trying to chat her up. Neil liked Dylan as a colleague. He was a good copper, but some of his comments about women made Neil's flesh crawl. The thought of him with Clare ... but Clare felt the same about Dylan and, anyway, she was nothing to do with Neil any more. Why then, when she called last night, had he felt a familiar flutter of the heart?

"You wanted to see me?"

Elizabeth Hayne was a tall, elegant woman who

looked more like a solicitor than a nurse.

"This is about the dead boy, isn't it? My husband told me about your visit. Then we saw the story in the evening paper last night."

Which indicated that he had nothing to hide.

"I'd like to show you a photograph," Chris said. Elizabeth Hayne looked at it.

"Yes, I'm pretty sure that that's the boy we saw being hit the other night."

"Was it a bad beating?" Dylan asked.

"Bad enough. If we hadn't come along there's no telling how serious it could have become."

"And you spoke to the victim?"

"Yes. He said that he thought the attacker was on drugs. I think we suggested going to the police, but he said he wasn't badly hurt. That was when Roger gave him our address, in case he changed his mind and needed a witness." Neil glanced at Dylan. Mrs Hayne had confirmed her husband's story, removing him as a suspect. But the couple could still be useful witnesses.

"What was the lighting like?" Neil asked.

"There was a street lamp up the road. I got a good look at the boy doing the beating. He was a long-haired youth, about the same age as the victim."

"Your husband was rather vague about the assailant," Chris went on. "Could you describe him in more detail?"

"I could try. I got a better look than Roger did. Roger's short-sighted, you know, and he wasn't wearing his glasses."

"Would you be willing to work with a police artist, see if you could come up with anything we could circulate?"

"Of course."

They paused. Sometimes, Neil's training said, a short silence asks a question for you. It gives the witness a moment to reflect, to think.

"Is there anything else you remember?" Dylan asked, gently.

Elizabeth pursed her lips before speaking.

"There is one thing. I got the distinct impression that the two boys weren't strangers to each other. I got the feeling that that was why he didn't want to go to the police, that we'd interrupted a private argument."

For once, Ruth's midweek days off coincided with Ben's. They had plans to drive into Derbyshire, go walking in the Peak District. If the mood took them, they would find a bed and breakfast, stay the night. Neither of them had to be back at work until two the following afternoon.

Ruth let herself into Ben's flat.

"You ready?"

As she reached the top of the stairs, she heard him speak curtly, then put the phone down.

"Trouble?" she asked.

"Wrong number."

Once they were in the car, Ruth asked whether Ben had heard anything about the murder. Instead of replying, her boyfriend slumped in the passenger seat of Ruth's 2CV.

"Cat got your tongue?"

"Sorry. I didn't sleep well last night – readjusting, you know."

"We don't have to go, not if you don't feel like it."

"No. It'll do us both good."

Ruth drove down the road, thinking.

"Is Charlene back at work yet?" she asked, out of nowhere, as they headed for the ring road. Ben's former girlfriend had been injured in a fire a few weeks before.

"I don't know," Ben said. "Why?"

"No reason. I'm just going to stop and get some petrol."

Ruth filled the tank. Ben insisted that they put the petrol on his credit card. He didn't have a car, but always liked to pay his way.

"Pick up an *Evening Post*, if it's out yet," she told him.

He came back with two tokens towards a free video tape and the first edition of the local paper. Scott Travis's photo was pasted across the front page. *Do you know this man?* the headline asked.

"Do you know him?" Ruth asked Ben.

"Why should I?"

"He was a character on your beat."

"I've never come across him before," Ben told her.

Ruth got him to read out the story. Things were in a sorry state when you got your information about a case from the newspapers.

"They're appealing for any information at all. CID haven't even been able to work out where the bloke lived yet."

"Does it say anything about motive?" she asked.

"Not a word."

Ruth wished that she had a part to play in the investigation. She'd like to discuss it with Ben, but he didn't seem interested. It was their day off, so maybe he had a point. Ruth put the radio on. They listened to classical music as they left Nottingham-shire. Soon they were driving through brilliant countryside, then parking by a pub which was reputed to do a superb beef in Yorkshire pudding. Ruth was glad, for a day at least, to leave crime far behind.

"Why do I still sleep with you?" Sam called from the bathroom.

"I don't think they call what we've just been doing 'sleeping'."

"Do you have *any* soap?"

"On the side of the bath. You do it because you

can't keep away from me."

"Ha!"

Sam picked up the paper she'd bought on the way back from work and threw it at Steve's tanned, muscular body. She liked him best when he was naked. He was right and he knew it. This was a physical thing. They were lovers, but they had never been in love. In a sense, they were using each other. But what was wrong with that?

"I do it because I'm sorry for you, more like. This soap is *disgusting*! Haven't you got a rehearsal to go to?"

Steve, since he packed in petty crime, had joined a small theatre group. They put on plays in pubs and other fringe-type venues, though Steve had yet to actually appear in one. Sam repeated herself.

"I said, have you got a rehearsal tonight? Because if you haven't..." She poked her head round the bathroom door and saw the look on Steve's face.

"What is it?"

Steve pointed at the photo on the front page.

"I know this guy."

"The one who got murdered?"

"Scott. His name was Scott."

"How do you know him?"

Sam walked back into the room. Steve looked upset.

"Tell me about him," she said.

"He's a ... *was* a small-time dealer. Scott knew

people who knew people. I went to his place a couple of times, trying to flog him stuff I'd nicked. But he never had any money. He'd give me some dope, or Es."

He paused and tried to chuckle.

"He was a mean sod, though. Never lost out on a deal. I once swapped him a video camera for an ounce of black."

Steve stopped, choking on his words.

"You seem to have been quite close to him."

"He was a sad bastard," Steve told her. "He wasn't a close friend or anything. I happened to have the time to listen to him, that's all. He always had plans, though I think even he knew that they weren't going to lead anywhere. He was a loser."

"And you know where he lived?"

Steve nodded.

"Aren't the police trying to find out his address?"

"Someone'll have told them by now. They don't need me."

"You ought to call them."

Steve didn't agree.

"I've had enough to do with the police to last me a lifetime."

"You owe them a favour or two," Sam argued.

Steve got out of bed.

"I don't owe anyone anything! If you want to tell them, fine. I'll give you the address. But I've got a rehearsal to go to."

* * *

Clare walked into the CID office at ten-past five. Neil was in there on his own.

"Dylan or Greasby around?" she asked.

"Dylan's at a parents' evening. The boss is on call."

"Have you found Scott Travis's address yet?"

Neil scrunched his eyes up, trying to work out what she was playing at.

"What is this? We've had a few calls, but none have panned out. Why?"

"You'd better get Greasby, then. I've found out where he lived."

"You're sure?" Despite himself, Neil looked impressed.

"I've got an informant who's ... who was a friend of his. He's sure. He was there only a couple of weeks ago."

"Informant..." Neil muttered, as he picked up the phone. "You mean Steve Garrett. He's the only criminal you know."

"You don't know what I've been up to since you left the shift," Clare told him frostily. "I knew Tracey Wicks, too. I make a point of getting to know people who might be useful. Though, yes, as it happens, we are talking about Steve, but not directly. I said I'd try to keep his name out of it."

"Fat chance," Neil said, putting the phone to his ear. "It's Neil Foster, boss. I've got an address for

Scott Travis. Think it's a definite." Clare passed him a slip of paper and Neil read it out.

"All right, yes. I'll meet you there."

He put down the phone.

"I suppose you'll want to come along?"

Clare gave him a sarcastic smile.

"The thought had crossed my mind. I did come in on my day off, after all." Neil was unimpressed.

"You could always have used the telephone."

"And missed the look on your face when I gave you the one piece of information you've been trying to get all day?"

"Come on," Neil said.

He checked out a car and got a crowbar from his locker.

"Actually," he told Clare, "there's another bit of information we're waiting for. A police artist is with a witness who interrupted some bloke beating up Scott Travis. Sounds like we might have a strong lead on the murderer."

Five minutes later they pulled up outside the address which Sam had given Clare.

"It's a squat," she told Neil.

"That'd explain why he's claiming housing benefit from somewhere else." They were on Birkin Avenue, off Radford Boulevard, five minutes' walk from the Forest. The terraced house had its windows boarded up and a sign informing the public that the place was coming up for auction in three weeks' time. Probably a building society repossession.

"Evidently you can get in through the back alley," Clare said. "He lived mainly upstairs. There's an extension in the attic and a skylight that isn't boarded up."

"The height of luxury."

"Are we going in then?" Clare asked, becoming impatient.

"We have to wait for the boss."

"What's taking him so long? Is he getting a search warrant?" Neil gave her a condescending look.

"This may or may not be a legitimate squat, but the squatter's dead and we're trying to find evidence against his murderer. I don't think anyone'll give a damn whether or not we've got a search warrant."

As they quarrelled, Greasby banged on the car window. He'd arrived without them noticing.

"Are we going in or what?"

Clare led them round the back as though she knew it well. In a sense, she did. She'd played in the back yards of many houses like this. Her parents still lived only three streets away.

There were deep scratches around the Yale on the back door.

"He's put a new lock in," Greasby commented. "A strong one."

Neil produced the crowbar. Clare and the inspector stood back as Neil smashed his way inside. Then they followed him upstairs.

The electricity didn't work. Clare had brought her torch but it was still hard to make out much. When they opened the attic door, however, a beam of sunlight dazzled them. Steep stairs led to a surprisingly airy loft extension.

The room was clean. A dust buster rested on the edge of a small Indian rug, covering a cardboard floor. A ghetto blaster and a tiny TV sat on the floor by the mattress, both battery operated. There was also a torch and a collection of prescription medication: sleeping pills, some kind of skin cream and a packet of anti-depressants. Greasby noted the doctor's name. In the sink was a pint of milk. It had gone sour, but was not yet mouldy. There were no pictures on the walls. The place had an unlived-in feel. It looked like the occupant wanted to be able to clear out in five minutes, taking all of his possessions with him.

They looked more closely. A cheap carry-all in a corner was full of dirty clothes. An examination of the bin yielded several beer cans and half a dozen cardboard roaches. There was nothing to indicate anything personal about the room's former resident, other than that he had trouble sleeping, liked to drink lager and smoke dope.

"All right," Greasby said. "I'll get some back-up over. We'll have the boards off the windows and take the place apart from top to bottom. Doesn't look too promising, though."

Clare felt disappointed. She'd brought them a big lead which had turned out to be going nowhere.

"Here," Greasby said to Clare. "I just collected this. Mean anything to you?"

He held out a photocopied drawing of a young man with a narrow, lined face, deep eyes and long, straight hair, badly cut. Clare shook her head. Greasby handed the picture to Neil.

"This is the picture that Elizabeth Hayne came up with."

Neil swore.

"I know this guy. I gave him a lift home the other night!"

6

Neil was a regular visitor to Wordsworth Hall, but the porter seemed surprised to see him.

"We need to see Max Walker," Neil announced. "Which is his room?" The man looked confused.

"D4, but he's not there. The students had to vacate their rooms by last Sunday."

Neil should have realized that, since he had helped Melanie move out, and half her stuff was in the attic room at his house.

"We're renting them out to conference guests now," the porter continued.

"You must have forwarding addresses for the students," Greasby said.

"Some of them."

They followed him to a small back office, where a

newly installed monitor showed everyone who came and went. The students' details were in a matt grey filing cabinet.

"Vasey, Violi ... Walker. He's not coming back next term. And there's no forwarding address, sorry. He should have filled in the form, but he hasn't. I can give you his parents' address."

"That'll have to do," Greasby said. "And we'd like to see his room."

The room was like all the others in Wordsworth Hall, square and nondescript, with a narrow single bed against one wall and a study desk and two shelves on the wall opposite. The room had been cleaned since the occupant vacated it.

"Waste of time," Neil said.

"Not quite," Greasby told him.

He pointed at the little black dots which marked the desk.

"Shows he's a pot smoker. Little lumps of hot hash fall out of the joint and burn the desk."

"Statistically," Clare pointed out, Miss Smart Arse, "half the students in the country smoke the stuff."

"Used to indulge yourself, did you?" Greasby teased her.

Clare ignored the jibe. For a year and a term, she had been a student in Manchester. Neil knew that she'd got up to a lot of things there which she preferred to keep quiet about in Nottingham.

"All I'm saying," Clare told the inspector, "is that the marks could be from one of the room's previous occupants."

"Maybe," Greasby said. "Let's go and ring his parents."

Neil remembered something as they walked down to the porter's office.

"Thinking about it, I've got a vague recollection that he said something about moving into a shared house."

"Now you tell us," Greasby moaned.

The DI was beginning to be in a bad temper. He was missing his dinner and they had turned up little of use. Nor did the phone call help. An answer-phone was on at the Walker household in Sevenoaks. Greasby didn't leave a message.

"Any more bright ideas?" he asked Neil.

"Max Walker can't be that hard to track down."

"Depends on whether he knows that we're looking for him."

"I could ring my girlfriend," Neil said, "see if she's got any idea where he moved to."

"You could do that," the DI said. "Call me at home if you get anywhere." Greasby got in his car and drove off.

"Need a lift?" Neil offered Clare.

"Hardly." Her house was only two minutes' walk away. "What did the pathologist's report say?"

That was Clare, wanting to know every last detail.

"Autopsy's not complete. All we've got so far is that it was a frenzied attack. Some kind of blunt instrument was used: a metal bar, a heavy piece of wood."

"DNA evidence?"

Neil shook his head.

"We're not going to get him that way."

"This student," Clare said, "Max Walker. What would be his motive?"

"You've got me there. Argument over money? We know very little about Scott Travis, other than he's dead, and no one seems to care very much. Now I've got to ring Melanie, then I'm going back to Birkin Avenue, see if I can help turn up anything in the search of the squat."

"Can I come with you?"

Neil had had enough.

"No! You're not in CID and this is your day off. I'm grateful for the tip, Clare, but this isn't your case. Back off."

Clare gave him a peculiar look and turned without saying goodbye. Neil had never been able to treat her so assertively when they were going out together. He felt pleased with himself for a moment. Then he worried, in case he'd hurt her. But there was no time to think about that now. He got in his car and drove round the corner. He wanted privacy when talking to his new girlfriend, and he would only get it by calling from his own home.

* * *

"I've missed you."

"Me too," Mel told him, her voice soft and breathy. "I'll come to stay next weekend, if you're not working."

"It depends on this murder case I'm on."

"Or you could come here..." She hesitated. "My mum 'n' dad'd like to meet you."

"My mum'd like to meet you, too, but I've told her there's no chance until we've been going out for at least three months."

"These things are different for girls," Melanie said. "Their parents worry more."

Neil didn't want to get into this now.

"I'm sure you're right," he said. "Listen, there's something I need to ask you. That bloke I gave a lift to the other day, Max. I need his new address."

"Why?"

Neil worded the reply carefully.

"Someone answering his description is mixed up in this murder we're investigating. I need to speak to him."

"I don't know where Max moved to. Sophie's more likely to have the address. She was kind of friendly with him. I'll get on to her if you like."

"Please."

The beeper in his pocket went off.

"Look, Mel, I've got to go. Miss you."

"Miss you too," she replied. "I'll call later, when

I've got through to Sophie."

"Found anything?" Neil asked the officer in charge of searching Scott Travis's squat. The boards were gone from the windows and the woodchip on the walls was seeing its first natural light of the year.

"Only this."

The officer handed Neil a white envelope which, from the post mark, must have come through the front door that morning. It was stiff to the touch and not properly sealed. Neil opened it. A cheap card was inside. On the front, pink teddy bears wished the receiver a happy birthday. Inside was a sentimental verse and a signature: *love, Karen.*

Somebody, somewhere, cared enough about Scott Travis to remember his birthday. Neil wondered who she was.

Clare stayed up late, listening to music. Funny how it had been her decision to finish with Neil, but now she was the one who was more upset. Every song seemed to have some kind of message for her. It stank. She had only had three real relationships in her life, and she'd been with Neil by far the longest – even though, or maybe because, she loved him the least. The first two guys had hurt her badly. But she seemed to have learnt nothing from any of these failures. She sometimes wondered if, where love was concerned, she had learned anything at all.

"On your own?"

Sam had come in from the pub. Clare gave a dour approximation of a smile.

"Ruth's stayed over in the Peaks with Ben. I didn't know where you were."

"I went for a quick drink with Steve after his rehearsal."

"I'm surprised you didn't go back to his place," Clare commented.

"You haven't seen his place. And I could hardly bring him back here, could I? Not after what…"

Sam no longer cared what Steve had done in the past, but her neighbours might.

"Who'd notice, after dark?" Clare asked.

"You would, for a start."

"I wouldn't mind."

In an odd sort of way, Clare liked Steve, even though he was a crook. Or maybe because he was a crook. She worked with crime. They had something in common.

"Don't worry," Sam said. "I like things just the way they are. Was that address helpful?"

Clare nodded, though she wasn't sure how much it had been, really.

"Did Steve remember anything else about Scott?" she asked, hopefully.

"We didn't discuss it."

"Anything at all might be useful," Clare said.

Sam hesitated.

"The only thing … I don't suppose it matters now, I mean … he got convicted, so…"

"Spit it out," Clare urged.

"When Steve was stealing, he used to pass the odd thing on to this Scott bloke. He'd swop them for drugs."

"I didn't know Steve was into drugs."

"He isn't – at least, no more than most people."

Most people Clare knew these days didn't take anything stronger than aspirin, but she didn't say this.

"What kind of things did he used to swop?"

"I don't know. You'd have to ask him. I think he mentioned a video camera."

Clare filed the information for future use. It wasn't worth passing on to CID. They already knew that Scott was, or had been, some kind of drug dealer. And if they wanted to interview Steve, they would.

At one, Clare went to bed, but found it hard to sleep. All kinds of things went round and round in her mind. Relationships. Murder. Her brother, Angelo, who would have finished school by now, if he were still alive. Random thoughts began to enter her head as she finally began to drop off. She had to see Paul Grace before she started her shift tomorrow, Clare remembered. What on earth was that about?

7

"Police. We've got a warrant. Open the door, please."

The best time to catch criminals at home, by common consensus, is early in the morning, before even the milkman arrives. Max Walker might not be a criminal, but CID weren't taking any chances. Three officers stood at the front of his Radford Boulevard House while a fourth was covering the back yard. They had a search warrant, just in case Max had the murder weapon concealed inside.

"For the last time, this is the police! Open up!"

Curtains parted in the windows of the houses on each side of the house they were trying to get into. These students would not be making a good impression on their new neighbours. Neil was worried.

Suppose he'd got it wrong? Suppose the man described by Elizabeth Hayne wasn't Max Walker?

From inside the house, there was the sound of a toilet flushing. Somebody thought they were the drugs squad. Dylan was about to smash the door in when it opened.

"Yeah? What is it?"

The long-haired youth at the door wasn't Max Walker, but that didn't stop the three officers charging into the hall. Neil found Max on the first-floor landing, wearing only boxer shorts. He was returning from the toilet. As the other officers began to search the house, Neil spoke to him.

"Get dressed, Max. We've got to take you in for questioning."

"This is about Scott Travis, right?" Max croaked. He had a sore throat.

"Right."

He almost looked relieved. For a moment, Neil thought that the student was going to confess, then and there.

"How did you know Scott Travis?" Greasby asked Max in the interview room.

"I met him last October," Max croaked.

He paused and a note of anxiety entered his voice.

"Look, you're only interested in the murder, right? Because if this is going to be about drugs, I want a solicitor."

"We're not interested in drugs," Greasby told him. "Just tell us everything there is to tell about Travis."

The story took a while, as Max's throat was so sore that he had difficulty speaking.

"Scott was in this pub where I'd been told it was easy to score. I bought an eighth of grass off him. It was lousy stuff. I wouldn't have gone back to him, but I'd told him where I lived. A couple of weeks later he came round, tried to sell me some more stuff. When I said I wasn't interested, he said that there'd be people who didn't like what I was getting up to. If I didn't buy his stuff, he'd tell them."

"And?"

"And I bought a couple of Es, just to get rid of him. But they were rubbish, too. I forgot about him after that. Beginning of next term, just after I'd cashed my grant cheque, he turns up again. This time it was threats straight away. 'Buy some stuff or I'm telling your tutor what you're up to.' Somehow he'd got hold of my pastoral tutor's name. I was worried. If Professor Dodd told the police and I got a conviction..."

Neil knew what he meant. With a drugs conviction, he'd never be able to practise as a doctor. Max went on.

"So I bought some puff just to get rid of him. The same thing happened a couple more times."

Detective Inspector Greasby spoke.

"Then, one day, you snapped, didn't you, Max?"

"What do you mean?"

Greasby nodded at Neil, who began to speak.

"It was the night I gave you a lift home from the Dodds'."

"So…?"

"So Scott was waiting for you, when you got home, wasn't he?"

"Yes."

"And he wanted more money."

"Yes." Max's voice was getting hoarser by the word.

"But you wouldn't give it to him."

"That's what happened."

"Did he threaten you?"

Max hesitated.

"I don't remember precisely. I'm not sure I gave him the chance."

"Because you beat him up."

"I wouldn't say that. I knocked him over, that's all."

"You hit him?"

Max's larynx had almost completely gone now. He was finding it hard to keep up the show of indifference.

"Once or twice," he croaked. "You know, I just wanted to get rid of him. I was meant to be going to the pub. I'd just taken some speed. I was angry. I wanted him to leave me alone."

"But you were interrupted."

"I think someone came. I'd already finished with him, anyway."

"You ran off."

"I wouldn't say I ran. Walked quickly, maybe. It was nearly last orders."

"Whatever. You were interrupted. So you waited ten days, then finished what you started."

"No," Max whispered, "that's not true. I never saw Scott again."

"I find that hard to believe, Max."

"You can believe what you want. You don't seriously think I killed him, do you?"

"Did you?" Greasby asked.

Max scowled.

"No, I didn't. I can prove it, too."

"How?"

"When did it happen?"

Neil and the inspector looked at each other. They could see no harm in telling him.

"Between eleven on Monday night and one on Tuesday morning," Neil said.

Max smiled. When he spoke, he'd got some of his voice back.

"I was in hospital, the Queen's Medical Centre, from lunchtime on Monday until four yesterday afternoon."

"Why?" Greasby asked.

"I was having my tonsils out. Why do you think I sound like this?"

Clare had just come on shift when the door to Inspector Grace's office opened.

"Clare? Could we have that word now?"

Uncomfortably, she joined the inspector. Grace looked ill at ease himself. He was a small, thin man, whose body sometimes seemed overwhelmed by an inspector's uniform. But he was a good policeman, Clare had discovered. He had earned the right to wear it.

"Have a seat, Clare."

She wondered what she'd done wrong.

"What's this about, sir?"

Grace hesitated.

"I need to ask you a favour."

"Of course, anything."

The inspector avoided meeting her eyes.

"You haven't heard what it is yet. And I want to make one thing clear – yes or no, this will have no negative or positive effects on your probation period."

"I see," she told him.

But Clare didn't see at all. She had no idea what the inspector was going on about.

"The thing is," Grace continued, unconsciously wringing his hands, "that it's Mess night the week-end after next." He paused, seeing Clare's blank face. "You do know what a Mess night is?"

Clare nodded. Mess night was a fancy affair, for

the ranks of inspector and above only. Posh, formal clothes were worn. A band played. It was, according to Jan Hunt, the place where senior officers did their most important networking.

"I've ducked out of two since I got promoted, but I can't miss another and I've bought two tickets. Thing is ... I don't have anyone to take."

Clare sucked in her cheeks. She hadn't been expecting this.

"Truth is, Clare, I'm a fairly solitary person. For one reason and another, I don't know many women. Especially single women. This is the big summer event at Epperstone Manor and, to a large extent, you're judged by who you take with you to these things. Do you follow me?"

Clare nodded. She understood that he was telling her the rumours were true. He was gay. The inspector had heard Clare shooting her mouth off and knew that she hated prejudice. He was counting on her to be sympathetic.

"I meant what I said when you sat down. I won't hold it against you in any way if you say 'no'. But you'd be doing me an enormous favour if you said 'yes'. And it could be to your advantage. You'll meet some people who might be very useful to you later in your career. I mean, you're obviously an ambitious woman."

"Yes, sir," Clare said. "I am."

"Will you?"

"I ... er..."

Clare didn't know what to say. The idea of going to a Mess night, when she had been in the force less than a year, was both exciting and daunting. That was one thing. The other was that people would assume she was going out with Paul Grace. She had promised herself never to go out with another police officer. This would only be pretend. It wouldn't count. But people would still talk.

"You don't have to give me an answer straight away," Grace said. "But..."

"But you need time to find someone else if I say no. Do you mind if I think about it, sir? I'm just a bit ... overwhelmed."

"Of course. Perhaps we could talk at the end of the shift?"

"Can we make it tomorrow? I'd like to – you know – sleep on it."

There was a knock on the door. Grace stood up. Clare made her escape as Jan Hunt came in.

"What was that about?" Ben asked Clare when she sat down next to him.

"I'll tell you another time."

Now Jan was back in the parade room, giving the afternoon briefing. She mentioned two missings from home, a mugging and, finally, the murder.

"A picture was circulated yesterday but the suspect has now been apprehended and cleared. So keep your eyes and ears open."

"Have we any idea what the motive for the killing was?" Gary asked. Jan shook her head.

"It's possible that the murder was drug related, but we have nothing definite. Now, Ben, I want you with me in the car today. Clare, go out walking with Gary."

Clare was disappointed. For once she'd hoped to be with Jan, to talk about the Grace thing. It wasn't right, putting the shift's two least experienced officers on foot patrol together. But it wasn't her place to argue. Gary collected the radios and they began their beat.

8

"So what was he?" DI Greasby asked, at the end of the day. "A drug dealer or a blackmailer?"

Two and a half days after the murder of Scott Travis, CID were no nearer finding out who had killed him, or why. Dylan tried to answer the question.

"The blackmail thing's not a runner, boss. If Scott was serious about blackmail, he'd have threatened to set Max Walker up – pay me now or I go to the police. Instead, he threatened the lad a little in order to sell him poor quality drugs. Technically, it might be blackmail, but I think we ought to be looking for a drugs angle. I mean, Travis obviously rubbed a lot of people up the wrong way. If someone like Walker can be driven to beat him up, then what would happen if he antagonized a real heavy? Didn't pay a bill perhaps?"

"You've got a point there. What do you think, Neil?"

Neil scratched his head. He very much wanted to impress the boss.

"I wonder whether there might be some kind of prostitution connection, sir. Given where he was found. Could Scott have been a rent boy?"

"Maybe. Or maybe someone wanted us to think that," Greasby commented. "After all, according to Forensic, there's nothing to show that the murder actually happened on Weston Avenue. No blood anywhere beyond the immediate area of the body. It's probable that the body was moved. But, presuming it was, there are no traces of the real murder scene on his skin or clothes."

"Did we check the house he was found by?" Neil asked.

"There was no sign of a break-in," Dylan told him. "I had a look through the windows. Nothing had been disturbed. Estate agents say it's been empty for months and the place looked it. Moreover, none of the street's residents heard anything. So it's likely that the killer drove over there, dumped the body."

"Does that get us anywhere?" Greasby asked Dylan.

"Not really. I guess the best we can do is get back

on to Vice and the drugs squad, have them rattle the cages of their informants. But my gut feeling is that we're on a loser with this one. If we don't get a witness…"

He let his words hang in the air. There was an unspoken feeling about this one, Neil realized. Scott Travis was scum and he'd been killed by more scum. It was what the older hands called a *slag on slag* murder. They'd try to find his killer, but they wouldn't bust a gut in the investigation. The dead boy wasn't worth it.

Tracey came in. She'd been out interviewing prostitutes.

"Get anywhere?" Greasby asked.

She shook her head.

"Want me to go out again tonight?"

"I don't think so," Greasby told her. "We'll have you and Neil back on the bogus callers tomorrow."

"Great. More waiting around all day."

"Prefer standing around on street corners, do you?" Dylan suggested.

Tracey gave him a contemptuous glance.

"So we've reached a dead end?" she said to the boss.

"There're a few people still to interview who responded to the newspaper and radio appeals. I'm seeing Travis's doctor today and we should get the full autopsy report. If that lot doesn't lead any-where, then we may have to move on to a more promising case," Greasby admitted. "At least until we get a new lead."

Neil drove home, disappointed. He was involved in his first murder case, but the whole thing seemed to have fizzled out in less than seventy-two hours. He had been hoping for more.

The end of the working day was a busy time for the women who worked the city's red-light zones. Kerb crawlers were at their worst now, slowing down the traffic, irritating local women who were mistaken for prostitutes. Clare thought it was worse for the parents walking their children home from school. Not long ago, kids arriving early at the local junior school had found a woman bleeding in the doorway. She had been knifed the night before by her pimp.

Clare felt sorry for the girls who worked these streets, but she had nothing but contempt for the punters.

"Why is it," she asked Gary, as they walked the streets of Hyson Green, "that men go to prostitutes?"

"I think that's the daftest question I've ever been asked," Gary told her. "It's the world's oldest profession. You've heard that?"

"I don't see what's so professional about selling sex," Clare said. "I understand what's in it for the women. They're desperate for money. But for the men ... how can they be so desperate for sex that they'll pay a stranger in some seedy, anonymous encounter? Don't they find it degrading? Are they that lonely?"

"Married, most of them are," Gary told her, jokily. "And some blokes find the whole seedy, anonymous bit a turn-on."

"Do you feel that way?"

Gary gave her a *we're getting a bit personal here* look.

"Sorry," Clare said.

They were passing the end of Hardy Street. A young girl in a pencil skirt and high heels was talking to another working girl who had just got into a car.

"Where're you taking him?" she was asking.

Satisfied by the answer, the young prostitute drew back and the car drove off. The girls looked after each other, Clare thought. But no one had been looking after Scott Travis.

"Hi, Sharon," Clare said. "I don't suppose you've heard anything about that bit of trouble a couple of night ago?"

"Nah," the young woman replied. "They got anyone for it yet?"

Clare shook her head.

"I seen him around, like. Whassisname? Scott."

"That's him. What did he do? Sell drugs?"

"Not to us, he wouldn't."

Sharon was kept in crack by her pimp. Clare tried to think of another question.

"Did Scott like girls?" Gary asked.

"Scott? I wouldn't know. Didn't talk to us lot much. I seen him with one girl a couple of times."

"What's her name?"

Sharon thought.

"They call her Cherie, but it's not her real name. She's on the game, but she don't work the beat any more."

"The beat" was what the girls called the area where they plied their trade.

"You think she was his girlfriend?" Clare asked.

"He wasn't hard enough to be her pimp."

Sharon looked at her watch.

"Look, do you mind? Only you're putting off trade and I need to earn another thirty before six."

That would be when her pimp came by.

"All right," Clare said. "But if you hear anything…?"

"I'll let you know," Sharon promised.

By the time they got to the top of Southey Street, Sharon had been picked up and another girl had taken her place.

"I'm impressed," Gary said.

"By Sharon? Your type, is she?"

"By you. You knew that girl. She trusted you."

"Part of the job, isn't it?" Clare said.

"When policemen get friendly with prostitutes, they usually only want one thing."

"That's gross," Clare said, shivering.

She knew that kind of exploitation went on, but didn't care to think about it. She and Gary walked briskly towards the Alfreton Road.

"It just saddens me," Clare said, "to see people selling something that ought to be so ... special."

"I know what you mean," Gary told her, "but you're not living in the real world. You talk as though sex is all about love."

"You're right," Clare admitted. "It's a mistake I've made before." She was surprised by how easy Gary was to talk with. He wasn't trying it on, either, which relaxed her.

"Can you keep a secret?" she asked Gary.

"Try me."

"Inspector Grace has asked me out."

Gary stopped and looked at her.

"Now that's a good secret," he said. "What did you say?"

She told him.

"Thing is..." she finished, "he only wants me there because I can be quite ... glamorous when I doll myself up."

"So I've heard. And he told you that he was queer?"

"Don't use that word," Clare said. "It's horrible."

Gary shrugged.

"No, he didn't," Clare said, "not in so many words. But it was clear that it isn't a proper date. It's for his career. What do you think I should do?"

"Go," Gary said. "And tell me all about it afterwards. After all, what have you got to lose?"

What indeed? Clare decided that she'd talk it over with Ruth before she made a final decision. Gary gave her his cheeky smile and Clare wondered whether it had really been wise to confide in him.

"What's life like at the YMCA?" she asked him. "Is it odd, living in a hall full of men?"

"Oh, it's unisex these days," Gary told her. "They've kept the old name, that's all. Although there are a lot more men than women. It's all right. I'm going to start looking for a place seriously soon."

"A bedsit?"

"Not if I can help it. I'd prefer a shared house. Misery likes company, that's me."

Clare nodded as though she understood. In truth, she couldn't quite make Gary out.

"Hi, Tracey," Gary called. "How's tricks?"

They went over to talk to the girl who'd found Scott Travis's body.

Jan was tired. Henry had thrown a tantrum this afternoon when she tried to take him over to Dawn's before work. The baby got on perfectly well with the childminder. Not long ago, he had taken his first steps at her house. But you couldn't expect a one-year-old to understand how his mother's shifts changed from day to day and week to week. Just when he was coming to count on her company, she was off again, and he wouldn't see her until the following morning.

Kevin was getting sick of it, too. He'd started to go quiet on her. For months after the baby was born, he'd suggested that Jan should go part-time – they could afford it – or get a desk job. He never seemed to understand that what she loved was nuts and bolts police work, not paper pushing. Recently, her husband had given up trying. He had even stopped discussing when they should have another baby. It was a bad sign. Hard to have a baby when they no longer had time for a sex life, Jan reflected. The weekend coming, Kevin was on call all the time. He saw even less of Henry than she did.

"Quiet period," Ben commented, as they drove through Lenton.

"What? Sorry, I was miles away."

"I was just saying how quiet it was. Would you mind if I stopped and made a personal call? It'll only take five minutes."

"No, of course not. Fine."

Jan could hardly complain. They had gone well out of their patch to check up on Henry earlier. He had, of course, been playing contentedly, no sign of his earlier trauma. Ben signalled right and turned into the Park. He pulled up outside one of the big old houses which had been divided into numerous flats.

"I'll be in C if anything comes through. Five minutes."

Jan nodded. She sat in the passenger seat, listening to the radio, thinking about Kevin. They had a fortnight's holiday booked next month, in Tenerife, which they sorely needed. Maybe it *was* time for them to make another baby. Henry deserved company. Sod the consequences to her career. The police force was only a job. She could take time out and come back in five years. Maybe.

The radio burst alive with a report of a sexual assault on Seely Road. Jan responded, noted the description of the attacker, then checked her watch. Ben had been gone ten minutes. She ran up the stairs and got to the door, just in time to see it open. A black woman who looked like a model was kissing Ben goodbye. Jan took a step back and said, "Ben. Quick! We're needed."

He hurried down to the car with a single-word apology and accelerated back on to the Derby Road. Jan said nothing. It looked like the mousy girlfriend who shared a house with Clare Coppola was on her way out.

"Over there!" she suddenly called to Ben, seeing a man hurrying across Derby Road to Rolleston Avenue. "He matches the description."

They set off in pursuit.

9

On Friday afternoon, Neil and Tracey were sitting on a landing at the top of Mr Bagley's stairs, waiting for a caller who probably wouldn't come.

"I can't imagine how he does it," Tracey said. "You don't just hand over money to people who turn up at the door."

"He's from a different age," Neil told her, "a time when people trusted each other, when no one committed crimes like this."

"An age that ended twenty or thirty years ago, only nobody thought to tell him."

"Yeah. But there have to be better ways to catch the con men than this." They were at the top of the stairs because it was the one place where they could see what happened at the front door without being seen themselves.

"There was a programme on the BBC a while back," Tracey commented. "South Yorks police installed a video camera in the victims' houses."

"And did the cameras chase the con men down the street and arrest them afterwards?"

"You've got a point," Tracey admitted.

"Do you want another cup of tea?" Mr Bagley called up the stairs.

"We're all right," Tracey insisted, loudly.

Making the tea was a big effort for him, and the last one had tasted disgusting. Neil got out the pack of cards. He and Tracey were playing pontoon for matchsticks. She'd won so many off him on Monday that he'd had to buy another box of Swan Vestas, average contents 85. But Tracey had been on CID for five years. She had a lot more experience than he did of playing cards. Neil began to deal. The doorbell rang.

Grace was late into the parade room that day. If Clare hadn't been catching up on some paperwork, before going out walking with Gary, she would have missed him. Gary was expected out of court at any minute.

"Afternoon, Clare," the inspector said as he walked through to his office. Clare glanced around. John Farraday was typing up a report. His partner, Tim, was off with his bad back again. John didn't have the best hearing in the world, and Clare spoke softly.

"What we discussed yesterday, sir. That'll be all right."

Grace's face lit up, but he spoke even more quietly.

"You're a lifesaver, Clare."

"How did it go?" she asked Gary when they started their beat. "It was your first time, wasn't it?"

"Changed his plea to guilty," Gary moaned. "I wasn't needed. What did you tell the inspector?"

"I told him 'yes'."

"And how did he take it?"

Clare shrugged.

"He seemed pleased. Why?"

"Only, I was thinking last night. Are you sure he's gay?"

"What are you on about?" Clare asked. "Look, I wouldn't have said anything if I thought you were going to turn it into gossip."

"It won't go any further, I promise," Gary said. "I'm the soul of discretion. But aren't I allowed to worry about you just a little bit?"

"In a word, no."

"Fair enough."

Clare changed the subject.

"Have you found anywhere to live yet?"

"I'm not in a hurry," Gary told her. "My room's a bit on the small side, but the guys I share a kitchen with are a good laugh. If I stay another few weeks I should be able to get a studio flat. I'd have my own kitchen and bathroom. Private intercom. My own TV if I want. Better than the accommodation at Ryton. And it's cheap."

"It sounds like being in a student hall of residence," Clare said.

"And what's wrong with that? You do get some students, but there're people with jobs, too. Quite a few homeless. All of life's rich pageant."

They walked along Forest Road West. The school was letting out. Gary smiled and waved at the little kids. That was his future, Clare decided. Gary would make a great community policeman. She wanted more from the job than that.

"Excuse me."

The woman standing in front of them was tall, about Clare's age, with a strong, familiar face and one of those long T-shirt dresses which Clare would like to wear, but they didn't suit her figure.

"Lost child, is it?" Gary said, smiling reassuringly.

Clare wouldn't normally have thought the woman old enough to have a child of school age, but, round this way, they started young.

"In a manner of speaking," she said. "It's about Scott Travis, the lad who was murdered. I was wondering if you could tell me what the arrangements are for his funeral."

"Oh."

"Only, I was a friend of his. He didn't have many. I'd like to go."

"Of course," Clare said, "we can find out. Gary'll radio for information." Clare paused, examining the woman's face.

"Excuse me, but don't I know you? Did you go to Greencoat school?"

"For a while, yes," the woman said, staring at Clare, trying to place her. "But I didn't go to school much from when I was about fifteen."

Suddenly, the face came into focus. Clare could picture the woman standing next to her six or seven years ago, in year-nine maths.

"Karen Cole."

"That's me. And you're … it's something Italian, isn't it?"

"Clare Coppola. How *are* you?"

"What about that! I was talking to the girls down the road. They said there was this WPC who was all right to talk to. Fancy it being you!"

"Let's walk," Clare said, suddenly getting a horrible suspicion of how Karen came to know Scott Travis. "We won't draw attention to ourselves." She nodded at Gary who, seeing that Clare wanted privacy, hung back. He was close enough to hear, Clare noted, but not near enough to disturb them.

The two women made small talk about their old

school for a couple of minutes, then Karen told her Scott's story.

"Scott and I were in a children's home together," Karen explained as they walked towards the Forest. "He got taken into care when he was four, me when I was five, so we arrived at the same time. I was like his big sister. We were both at the Barrack House, in Aspley, on and off. That was why I went to Greencoat. So did Scott, but he was in the year below and skived off a lot, so you wouldn't remember him. Then they closed that dump down and we got moved to Holyleigh in St Ann's."

Clare knew what was coming next.

"Most of the girls in that place were on the game. Some as young as thirteen. There were always older blokes hanging about outside, offering rides, drugs, places to stay. Well, I was fifteen and not bad-looking, so I was snapped up. Neville, his name was. Told me he loved me. Had me working the streets within a month.

"I'd get picked up by you lot now and then, sent back to Holyleigh. I was always going on to Scott about what a good time I had. He stayed with me a couple of times when he did a runner from Holyleigh himself. Then he stopped going back."

"How did he live?" Clare asked.

"Just moved around, did whatever he could to get by. Dealing drugs mostly. He started by delivering, then learnt to skim off a bit and sell it for himself.

One time, he got caught, beaten up. He came to stay with me and my baby. I've got a two-year-old, Timmy. Scott loved to play with him. I patched Scott up, told him not to take silly risks. That was six months ago."

"When did you see him last?"

"At the weekend."

"Last weekend?"

"On Sunday, yes."

That made her the last known person to have seen Scott alive.

"He came by, told me things were going really well. He was getting into something new."

They had stopped now at the end of the avenue where Scott's body had been found. Karen didn't seem to notice.

"What kind of thing?" Clare asked.

"He didn't say. I thought it probably had something to do with drugs. One time he was going on to me about how easy it was to make your own Ecstasy. He was living in this squat and I warned him not to try anything dangerous. He could be a bit soft in the head, Scott."

Karen shook her head from side to side. A single tear trickled down her left cheek.

"Fifteen years I've known him," she said, softly. "Every single thing he's ever done ended up backfiring on him."

10

"That's it, I'm cleaned out."

"You're a lousy gambler, Neil Foster."

"My problem is, I'm too much of an optimist."

"Got a good weekend lined up, optimist?"

Neil smiled.

"Melanie's coming to stay. We'll probably — you know — have a quiet time."

"Oh, yeah? I wish my boyfriend and I were still at the 'you know' stage." They both laughed. Downstairs, the home help who had turned up an hour before was saying her goodbyes.

"Will you be here next time, duck?" she called up to Tracey.

"I don't know. Like I said before, if you see anything suspicious, call me on…"

The beeper which Neil kept in his left trouser-pocket began to vibrate. He checked the number which came up on the tiny screen. A message came up to call DI Greasby.

"Better go down the road."

Mr Bagley was in one of the nine per cent of houses in the country which didn't have a phone.

"Don't be long," Tracey said. "We're due to finish in twenty minutes." Neil opened the front door and hurried out into the street, nearly knocking over a florid-faced man who was about to knock on the door. The man was wearing what, at first glance, looked like a council worker's jacket. He took one look at Neil, then another at the home help, who was putting on her coat and saying to Tracey, "Well, I hope you catch him."

Then the fake council worker said, "Sorry, wrong house," and got back into his car before Neil could react. Neil yelled up to Tracey, then banged on the car window.

"Hold on, I want a word with you."

Too late. The car was already moving. Neil, cursing, took its number, doubting that the information would be of much use. They had no evidence to prosecute the guy. The whole surveillance had been wasted.

The message said that a new witness had been found in the Scott Travis case, a prostitute called

Karen Cole. Dylan was off sick today. They were the only people available to interview her. Neil and Tracey drove to the address given.

"Look at this," Neil said, as they pulled up and parked next to a BMW. "It looks like we're in the wrong job."

"Speak for yourself," Tracey told him.

Karen Cole had a flat near Mapperley Road, in a modern building. Neil wasn't surprised to find Clare there, waiting for them. She seemed to be constantly getting underfoot in this case. He hoped that, this time, her information got them somewhere.

The living room was big, with chairs for four of the five people in it. Gary, Clare's new partner, having nowhere to sit, went to make them all a cup of tea. Tracey conducted the main interview.

Karen worked from home, she explained. The men came to her through contact magazines and passed-on phone numbers. She called herself Cherie. The flat had a private, secluded entrance, which made her profession easier. Karen didn't want the neighbours knowing what she did for a living. Only one person knew, a woman with a flat in the next-door house, who used to be on the game herself. She looked after Timmy when Karen was working.

Karen pointed to the mantelpiece.

"That's me and Scott."

The photograph showed a pretty, prepubescent

girl and a cheeky-looking, fresh-faced boy, their arms around each others' shoulders. They were in jeans and T-shirts, standing on a beach somewhere.

"Day trip to Skeggy," Karen said. "Lovely day. Only trouble was, we none of us had any swimwear. Home hadn't thought of it, so they wouldn't let us go in the sea. Not that any of us had ever learnt to swim."

She told them the story of Scott's life, as far as she knew it. He was taken into care when he was four. Mother was a single parent, who couldn't or wouldn't protect the child from a violent boyfriend. She had stopped visiting when Scott was six. The boy had been fostered three or four times, the last when he was ten. But the placements never worked out and he always ended up back in the home, as did she. Both of them left the home a year before they were supposed to be able to, at fifteen.

"And Scott became a drug dealer?"

"He delivered drugs for a while, when he was young enough not to get a prison sentence. Then he went on to selling them. He got caught last year. The other day, I told him he was lucky to have got away with it for so long, that he ought to get a job. He said not to worry, he was working on a way to get out of dealing. He had this idea for doing something more profitable."

"This was the last time you saw him, the Sunday before he died?"

"Yes."

"What else did you talk about?"

"What does anyone talk about? Other people, I suppose. There was this girl we both knew, used to be on the game. She got married recently. He'd seen it in the paper; said she looked pregnant in the photograph. He was funny like that, Scott. Always picking things up. When I used to work on corners, I'd sometimes see him, watching."

"Were you ... intimate?" Tracey asked.

"You mean lovers? No. Scott was like a little brother to me. Anyway, I'm pretty sure that he was gay, even though he was too young to realize it. I took him to clubs a few times. They're really safe, friendly places for a woman like me, gay clubs. Scott was a bit wide-eyed at first, but he seemed comfortable. It was only a matter of time before he came out to himself."

"Did he talk about any other friends?" Neil asked.

"There was one bloke he was friendly with. The way he talked, I reckon Scott had a crush on him. Trouble was, the bloke turned out to be straight. I'm afraid I can't remember his name."

"Steve Garrett?" Clare suggested.

"That was him."

I might have known, Neil thought. The officers looked at each other.

"Can I ask something?" Clare said.

Tracey nodded.

"Did Scott say anything to you about a video camera?"

Karen shook her head.

"Do you know if he had one?"

"He didn't mention it to me. I can't see what he'd do with one of those. He had trouble turning on a TV, Scott did."

As the officers got up to go, Karen asked, "I wanted to know about Scott's funeral."

"It won't be for at least a fortnight," Tracey said. "Thing is, if we find the murderer within that time, his defence is entitled to a second autopsy. Sorry."

"What was all this about a video camera?" Neil asked, as they were leaving.

Clare seemed embarrassed.

"I thought you knew. The one Scott got off Steve Garrett, a month ago."

"This is the first I've heard of a video camera."

"I don't know why Scott wanted it. That's why I asked Karen."

Neil and Tracey looked at each other.

"We'd better make another full search of the squat where Travis was staying," Tracey said. "I'll get over there. Neil, why don't you track down this Steve Garrett, bring him in to the station?"

Neil dropped off Tracey, then gave Clare and Gary a lift back to their beat.

"Steve won't be home," Clare told him. "He's

working on this play they've got in rehearsal at the Arts and Crafts Centre."

"Thanks, Clare," Neil told her, looking at his watch. He should be coming off shift in five minutes. Fat chance. "Enjoy your weekend."

Steve was wearing a dusty tracksuit when Neil spotted him, and seemed to be in the middle of a speech. Seeing Neil, Steve stopped in mid-sentence, apologized to the director, then said he'd be with Neil at the end of the scene. When he did, he looked disgruntled.

"What's this about?" Steve asked.

"I'm afraid I need to take you to the station with me."

"We open next month," Steve complained. "And we're way behind. I can't let people down."

"I'll run you back as soon as we've finished with you. I can't say fairer than that."

Steve went and explained to the others, who adjourned to the pub.

"I'm in every scene," he told Neil. "They can't do much without me. Still, if this helps find out who killed Scott... Why is it you want me again?"

"We're interested in a video camera you forgot to mention selling to Scott."

"I didn't sell it," Steve protested, "I..."

"What?"

"Never mind."

* * *

Clare finished her shift at ten. She was about to go for a bus when Grace popped his head around the parade room door.

"Need a lift, Clare? I'm just off myself."

"Thank you, sir."

Two members of the oncoming shift gave her funny looks. As a rule, constables didn't get lifts from inspectors. But Clare didn't care what they thought.

The front seat of Grace's car was far comfier than the back.

"Eventful day?" the inspector asked.

"I managed to bump into Scott Travis's oldest friend."

"Really? That was good luck."

Clare told herself off. She should have made it look like detection, rather than luck.

"Yes," she told Paul Grace. "It turned out I was at school with her."

"And did she shed any light on the motive for the boy's murder?" Grace asked, keeping his eyes on the road ahead.

"Not really. The only substantial new bit of information was that Karen reckoned Scott was gay. However, as far as she knows, he never had a relationship."

Clare waited for the inspector's reaction, but Grace made no comment. The lights changed, and they headed down the hill.

"This thing next Saturday," Clare said. "What should I wear?"

"Nothing too daring," Grace told her. "A black cocktail dress would probably be safest. Have you got something like that?"

"Sure."

"And simple jewellery. Nothing ostentatious."

"I don't think I own anything ostentatious," Clare told him.

"I do appreciate this, you know," Grace added, turning into her street.

"And I appreciate the lift," Clare said. "Have a good weekend, sir."

"We're off-duty now. It's Paul."

"Goodnight, Paul."

"Goodnight, Clare."

Back in the house, Clare changed hurriedly and headed to the Carlton for last orders. When she got there, she wished she hadn't. Ruth was sitting with Sam and Steve.

"Two hours they kept me there!" Steve complained. "Completely destroyed our rehearsal. As if I'd know what he was up to with that video camera."

"They haven't found it, then?" Clare asked.

"Doesn't sound like it. I told them, I gave him the camera just the way I got it. Sony camcorder, ten-times zoom, that's all I remember. No case. Video 8 tape inside. One battery and one battery charger.

They expected me to remember what model it was, where I got it, the lot. Threatened to charge me."

Clare sighed.

"I mean, I was only trying to help, wasn't I?"

Sam looked embarrassed. At times like this, Clare couldn't understand why she went out with him. Steve turned to Clare.

"He wasn't very technological, Scott. I had to teach him how to use it. But he never told me what he wanted it for. Why wouldn't they believe me?" Clare wasn't sure how much CID had told Steve. She didn't want to give anything away.

"Blue movies?" she suggested to Steve.

Steve shook his head.

"Scott never talked about sex. I reckon he was using it for some kind of surveillance. He went on about how to use the autofocus and how low lux it was."

"*Lux?*" Clare asked, bemused.

"Yeah. It was a one-lux camcorder. Gave a really clear image at night. Scott wanted to be sure that he could set the camcorder up anywhere and leave it filming."

"And why would he want to do that?" Clare asked.

"Search me," Steve said.

11

"I was looking forward to going home," Melanie said, "especially after all the horrible things that happened last term. Now I'm there I keep wishing that I was back in Nottingham. Weird, eh?"

"Not so weird," Neil said, squeezing her hand.

They were walking through the Arboretum on Saturday afternoon. The sun was out and the park's green lawns were sprinkled with young couples.

"I've been doing lots of work for my course next year. We got this summer reading list which assumes you've got the time to go through thirty books."

"What do you do," Neil asked, "skim them?"

Melanie laughed.

"I've tried doing that, looking for the good bits, but it doesn't work. You have to try and immerse yourself in them. Do you know what I mean?"

"I guess."

Neil couldn't really relate to someone spending all their time reading books and writing about them, but it didn't matter. It made a change from talking about police work.

"Do you think I should go and see Max?" Melanie asked, as they rounded the bandstand.

"Why? To make sure he's over his operation?"

Max Walker might not be guilty, but he had some unsavoury contacts. Neil wasn't happy about Melanie hanging around with him.

"No. But, I do know him. And it must be pretty horrible, when someone you know gets murdered."

Neil thought that Melanie's sympathy was misplaced. "Believe me," he told her, "Max did not like this guy."

Melanie sighed.

"I won't ask you to come with me."

"I would if you wanted me to," Neil said. "I don't think Max would appreciate it, though."

"You're sweet," Melanie said, kissing him.

Hand in hand, they walked towards Waverley Street and the coming evening.

"If you hadn't turned Neil down you wouldn't be spending Saturday nights with us, wasting time on terrible movies," Nick Coppola told his daughter as they watched a second-rate Clint Eastwood on Central TV.

"I couldn't marry him, Dad. I wasn't in love with him."

"In that case, why did you go out with him for the best part of two years?"

"Nick, leave her alone!" Maria Coppola interrupted. "Clare, tell us about this dance you're going to next Saturday."

"It's just a work thing."

"And this man you're going with is an inspector," Dad pointed out. "I thought you said you were through with dating policemen?"

"It's not a date," Clare insisted, although, technically, that was exactly what it was. She certainly wasn't going to explain about Paul Grace being gay. Dad thought that homosexuality should still be illegal.

"What is it then?" Mum asked.

"Look, can we leave it?" she said. "He asked me to go as a favour. Strictly no strings. And it'll be useful to me. Don't go on about it. I'm nervous enough already."

"All right," Mum said. "I'm ready for bed. You want me to make up a bed in your old room, Clare, stay here tonight?"

"No, I'm going to walk home in a minute."

"The streets aren't so safe," Dad warned her.

"I'm a police officer," Clare reminded him. "I can look after myself."

Outside, the *For Sale* sign still stood. Mum and

Dad were talking about taking the house off the market. They could no longer really afford to move. Dad's building business had failed to revive in the spring. It was barely ticking over. Clare would be happier if they remained on Berridge Road West, a short walk from her new home. Upstairs, though, her brother's room remained untouched, like a shrine. If they stayed put, that would have to change.

Walking on to Gregory Boulevard, Clare glanced up at the other side of Birkin Avenue, where Scott Travis used to live. Then she stopped. Someone was turning into the alley which led to the back of his house.

There was no reason for anyone to be going to the terrace where Scott Travis used to squat. They must be going to the house next door. Clare walked up the street nevertheless. Scott had fitted a new lock to the back door. What if someone else had a key? Clare stepped into the alley. She was mad, she knew that. She didn't have her torch, or a truncheon. She wasn't in uniform. But it would only take a minute to find out.

Taking care to be quiet, she walked to the end of the alley. The houses at either side were in darkness. Clare went into the yard of the one where Scott used to live. The boards had been removed from the windows and not replaced, but she could see no light inside. The lock on the back door was still broken from when Neil used the crowbar on it.

Clare pushed the door open and listened.

There were noises, coming from upstairs. Cautiously, Clare walked into the back room. She felt her way around, remembering the layout from her previous visit. As her eyes adjusted to the lack of light, she opened the door at the bottom of the stairs. Then, slowly, she began to climb them, making as little noise as possible.

Whoever was inside had walked up to Scott Travis's attic room. Maybe they were only sleeping there, Clare thought. It could be another squatter. She would snatch a look, then get out as quickly as possible. No, she decided, as she reached the top of the stairs, it was too risky to go inside. She would listen.

The door was slightly ajar. Clare could hear a man moving about the room, swearing. Clare took a step back. She should never have come in here. If she went back down, got to a call box, a patrol car would be round in two minutes. This was a job for someone in uniform.

Clare took another step back. The door flew open and a torch shone in Clare's eyes, dazzling her.

"Who are you?" asked the big, dark figure behind the light in a deep, booming voice. "What the hell are you doing here?"

12

Neil and Melanie were in bed when the phone rang.

"Don't answer it," Neil said, as his girlfriend moved away from him. "It's gone midnight."

"And what if someone's died?" Melanie asked, reaching out of the bed. She picked up the phone, said the number, and listened with a frown on her face.

"It's your ex," she told Neil, handing him the receiver. "Again. Doesn't she have a life?"

Clare sounded excited.

"Sorry, I know it's late, but I had to tell someone. I've found a witness! I know where there's a video-tape! I think I know why Scott Travis was murdered!"

"Jesus, Clare, calm down," Neil said. "What are you on?"

"I'm sorry. Is this a bad time? I had to tell some-body. The thing is, we need to take a statement off this bloke as quickly as possible."

Neil nearly told her to ring Dylan. The DS lived alone. He'd be thrilled to hear from Clare on a Saturday night, Neil was sure. Then he remembered that Dylan was off work ill.

"All right, I'm coming. Where are you?"

"At home."

"I'm on my way."

Melanie groaned as he put the phone down.

"I'm sorry," he told her as he dressed. "It does sound very important."

"It better be." She got out of bed. "I may as well come with you. I'll never get to sleep here on my own."

She looked at Neil, seeing that the idea made him uncomfortable.

"Go on then. Go without me. But please don't be long. We've only got tomorrow, then I won't see you for at least two weeks. It's not fair."

"It's not," Neil agreed, knowing that, if Clare's information was as big as she said it was, he'd probably have to go into work all day tomorrow. "See you later."

He picked up his warrant card and car keys from the dresser and blew her a kiss as he walked out of the door.

* * *

"This is Tricky," Clare said, introducing Neil to the Rasta on the sofa. "He was Scott Travis's dealer. I've told him that we're not interested in drugs, that we only want to find out who killed Scott. That's right, isn't it?"

Neil grimaced at Clare. She could tell that he was still angry at being called out. Clare knew that what she'd said was true: CID made deals like that all the time. Technically, however, Clare wasn't in a position to make any offers. She wasn't even on duty. But Neil played along with her.

"That's right," Neil said, smiling at the guy in order to try and gain his trust. Tricky was in his early twenties, overweight, and wore round, tinted glasses.

"Tricky was in Scott's squat earlier," Clare explained. "I interrupted him searching the place."

It had been a hairy moment. If she'd been dressed in a police uniform, Tricky might have hurt her. He would certainly have fled. But Clare had managed to talk to him, to plead for his help in solving Scott's murder.

"Could you tell Neil what you told me, please?" she asked him.

The fat Rasta spoke. Tricky might have sounded scary when he confronted her earlier, but his normal speaking voice was as gentle as that of a priest in the confessional.

"Scott was my friend, right? I used to supply him

every now and then. Small stuff, you understan'? I'm not big time."

"When did you last see him?" Neil asked.

"The day he died."

"Do you know who killed him?"

Tricky shook his head.

"If I did, I would have told you, man. Like I said, Scott was a friend. I'd like to see whoever done it put away. No, I don't know who killed him. But I do know what got him killed."

"What?" Neil asked, not sure whether he was being wound up or not. Tricky told Neil what Clare had teased out of him earlier.

"Blackmail. That was Scott's new game. He had things on people."

"What kind of things?"

"I don't know all of it. I don't have *details*."

Neil began to look exasperated. Clare knew what he was thinking. He was wondering if Clare had got him out of bed only to waste his time. She hadn't.

"Then what *do* you have?" Neil asked.

"All I know is: Scott asked me to look after his video camera for him. He said that he was getting into this blackmail thing. He didn't want anybody to be able to follow him home, steal the tapes off him. Also, I knew how to transfer tapes, make copies for him."

Neil began to look interested.

"Did he tell you what kind of secrets he knew about his victims?"

"Sure." Tricky smiled, enjoying making Neil wait. "One used to be a street walker, right? Didn't want her husband to know. One was a medical student, didn't want his teachers to know he was using. Some guy was cheating on his wife, or girlfriend, something like that, right? And then there was a policeman. Young guy."

That got Neil. He exchanged a concerned glance with Clare.

"What policeman?" Neil asked.

"He didn't tell me any names. He didn't even tell me what he had on the police guy, only that he had it, right?"

Neil nodded.

"And he told you all this because you were looking after his camcorder?"

"Right."

"So where is it?"

Tricky shrugged.

"The video camera? I don't know."

Neil sighed and looked at Clare. His *I'm losing patience* look.

"Tell him why," Clare told Tricky.

"Monday afternoon, Scott comes to see me, says he needs the video camera. He stays around a while, charging the battery up, puts a new tape in. We talk a little. He says he'll be back around midnight. But he never shows up. Next day, I hear he got killed."

"Why didn't you come forward earlier?" Neil

wanted to know.

Tricky didn't answer. If he had come in the day after the murder, CID could have saved five days of digging around for a motive. But the drug dealer wasn't the sort of person who went to the police voluntarily. It probably hadn't occurred to him that the police cared one way or another how Scott came to die.

"Why were you in the squat tonight?" Neil asked, having given up on getting an answer to the previous question.

"I didn't know the police knew where it was, right? Thing is, Scott owed me money. I thought I'd take some of his things, sell them. They're no use to him where he is, right? But they were all gone. Then this girl comes upstairs. She's telling the truth, right? She is police?"

"Oh, she's telling the truth all right," Neil said, then looked at Clare. "I thought you said you had the video camera? He says that Scott took it."

"Not the camera," Clare told him, "a tape."

"Right," Tricky added. "I still have the charger and Scott's spare video tape."

"Is there anything on it?" Neil asked.

He was starting, at last, to seem excited.

"Yes. Some guy leaving a woman's house. Scott had me make a VHS copy for him last week."

"To show to his victim?"

"You got the idea."

"Where's this tape?"

"Back at my flat."

"I guess I'd better phone DI Greasby," Neil said. "He's not going to like being woken up."

"This isn't going to take long?" Tricky asked, when Neil was out of the room.

"Not long now. A few minutes. They'll probably want you to make a formal statement tomorrow."

"Only I have a few calls to make, right?"

"I understand."

Clare didn't like to think what drugs Tricky had concealed about his person. Neil came back.

"All right, let's go."

"I'll get my coat," Clare said.

"I don't think so," Neil told her.

"What?" Clare couldn't believe her ears. "I just found…"

"There's nothing for you to do," Neil interrupted.

"I want to see what's on the tape."

"We won't be able to look at it until tomorrow," Neil told her, "not unless you've got the same make camcorder about the house. And, anyway, Tricky here's told us what's on it. A man leaving a place where he shouldn't be. The inspector told me to collect the tape and meet him in the office at nine tomorrow."

"I'll be there," Clare told him.

"No, you won't," Neil said, dismissively. "Look,

I appreciate the help, Clare, but it's not your case. Let it go."

Neil led Tricky out to his car. Clare watched in silence, fuming. It seemed that no matter how much she helped with the investigation into Scott Travis's murder she was always going to be left on the sidelines.

13

"What do you reckon?" Ruth asked, late on Sunday morning.

They were sitting in Ben's flat, surrounded by brochures she'd picked up in town the day before. After their day out in the Peak district, Ben had suggested that they take a foreign holiday together and Ruth had jumped at the idea. However, there weren't as many last-minute bargains to be had as they'd hoped.

"If we wait until September," Ruth tried again, "we'd have a bigger choice."

"I was thinking more of sometime in August."

"Yeah, but it's practically August already, and September's such a depressing time. It makes me think of going back to school and nothing really to look forward to until Christmas."

"I dunno," Ben said. "I just wanted to get away as soon as possible."

"Why?"

Not for the first time, Ruth got the feeling that Ben was acting strangely. Was there something that he wanted to run away from?

"Why not? How do you feel about that week in Turkey?"

"Unconvinced. I'd prefer Spain, or Portugal."

"More expensive."

They tossed the options around for another twenty minutes, not getting anywhere. Theirs was an equal relationship, Ruth thought, the most equal she'd known, because they were both willing to listen to the other and look for a compromise. Which didn't always mean that they found one.

"Maybe we should leave it for today," Ruth said.

The phone rang. Ben answered it.

"Yeah. I understand. Next time. Fine. Good luck." Ben turned to Ruth. "That was Neil." They were meant to be going out for a drink with Neil and Melanie that night. He went on. "They've got a load of new leads in the Scott Travis case."

"I know. Clare told me."

"Thing is, Neil's at work. Melanie's gone home. Drink's off."

"What shall we do instead? There's this film on at the Savoy…" Before Ruth could finish, the phone rang again. Ben picked it up and listened for a few seconds.

"No. You've got the wrong number."

Later, when Ben was having a shower, Ruth reached over to the phone and dialled 1471, the digits which give you the number of the last person who called. She listened to the computerized voice speak the number twice, memorized it, then put the phone down.

"So this is where you live?"

Clare had tracked Gary down at the YMCA. Gary had been called down via the intercom. Luckily, he was home. She'd needed someone to discuss the Travis case with. Ruth had spent the night at Ben's and not returned yet.

"This is it," Gary said. "I'd show you my room, but it's a mess, and the other guys are up there."

"Whatever," Clare told him. They were standing at the bottom of the steps on the second floor, by the office, opposite the restaurant. The place was full of brown wood. It was like stepping into a time warp. Clare tried to guess the period when it was built. Probably the fifties or early sixties. Clare looked about her. People came and went, most of them about her age. It seemed odd that there was this whole other world in the middle of town, one she hadn't noticed before.

"Fancy a bit of lunch?" Gary suggested. "I haven't eaten yet."

"Why not?"

Clare hadn't been able to face going to her parents for Sunday dinner. She joined Gary in the food queue and insisted on paying for dinner herself. She could sense his awkwardness around her, out of uniform. People he knew were glancing at him, as if to say, *so that's Gary's girlfriend*. Maybe she shouldn't have come.

"Just like school dinners," Clare said, eating hungrily.

"You can't have gone to my school. These are *cordon bleu* by comparison. So tell me, to what do I owe this pleasure?"

"I found out why Scott Travis was murdered," Clare told him, with a grin.

"Do tell."

Gary stopped eating and smiled.

"Because he was a blackmailer."

The smile left Gary's face and he turned pale.

"Are you all right?"

Gary gulped down some water.

"It's nothing, bit of food went down the wrong way when you said that. Tell me everything."

She did. When Clare got to the bit about one of Scott's victims being a policeman, Gary asked for more details. But Clare didn't have any for him.

"Want to do something?" she asked Gary when they'd finished eating. "It's a lovely day. We could go for a walk in the Arboretum, if you like."

116

Gary looked at his watch.

"Hell, I'm sorry," he said. "I'm supposed to be meeting someone. I mean, I'm really glad you came round to see me, but..."

"It's OK," Clare said.

He was obviously lying.

"Come and visit me sometime," she added.

"I'll do that," Gary said, with an apologetic smile. "See you tomorrow."

"Yes. Tomorrow."

Clare walked back through the Arboretum anyway. They were having a long, hot summer and she wanted to enjoy the weather. However, it seemed everybody else she saw was in a couple. Clare felt low. It wasn't that she was desperate for a romance. She wouldn't mind being on her own so much, if only she could get some credit for helping in the Travis case.

She wondered why Gary suddenly became so uptight just now. Had she said something to upset him? Clare was annoyed that he'd got rid of her that way. She liked Gary. He seemed to like her. For once, couldn't she simply get on with a guy and be good friends with him? Just once would be nice.

14

After a breakthrough on a case, there's a feeling of energy, a rush of inspiration which makes the boring bits of the job seem worthwhile. But, without results, the feeling doesn't last. By Sunday afternoon, Neil and the other CID officers on duty felt like they were banging their heads against a brick wall. Tricky had given his statement but, so far, it had turned out to be less helpful than they'd first hoped. True, they knew that Scott Travis was a blackmailer, but, unless there was a miraculous revelation on the videotape, how were they to find his victims?

One was a policeman. Twenty-five officers worked Nottingham West, the area where Scott lived, a figure that you could double if you included the adjoining patch known as South. Add another ten if you counted the CID officers who covered both areas. Where did you begin with them?

Then there was an ex-prostitute. Such women weren't easy to find. For a start, many women tended to drift in and out of prostitution, depending on their economic and domestic circumstances. Secondly, if a woman had married and taken her husband's name, there was no simple way of tracking her down. The data protection act made it illegal for the police to go through the most obvious routes, the DSS and National Insurance computers. You could track the woman back through her parents, perhaps, if they still lived locally, but that was a time-consuming and embarrassing process. Over a thousand different prostitutes had been convicted in the last five years.

It was also possible that Scott was blackmailing a man he'd had a homosexual relationship with. If so, they had no leads there, either. The man couldn't have been convicted of a connected offence which the police could check up on. Otherwise, why would Scott be able to blackmail him?

That left the man who was cheating on his wife or partner. According to a women's magazine survey Neil had looked at in the dentist, the vast majority of men and a smaller majority of women cheated on their partners at least once. They were looking, therefore, at about half of the adult population. But at least they had a video. DI Greasby was examining it at the moment.

Where to start? Neil had an alphabetical list of prostitutes arrested in the last five years, together with their most recent known addresses. He read down it, hoping to find familiar names. Karen Cole was on there. She ought to be reinterviewed. The letters from D to Z, however, revealed nothing at all.

Tracey returned from a block of flats in Radford, the one where Scott Travis had been claiming his benefits from, even though he didn't live there.

"Anything?" Dylan asked, his voice still full of the cold that had kept him off work on Friday.

"We upset a few people," Tracey told him, "but we didn't find a sausage."

Greasby came out of his office, accompanied by a young bloke in a plain white shirt and blue jeans. Neil recognized him. Gary something. He'd been partnering Clare recently.

"Gary's come in to give us a hand," Greasby told the others. "He knows the area. Chris, take him with you. Tracey, you and Neil can do the working girls again. Get anywhere with that list of names, Neil?"

"Not a chance."

"Never mind. It was a long shot. Out on the streets, both of you. Chris, in here."

While Dylan went into the inspector's office, Gary sat down and waited. What was he doing here?

Neil wondered. Gary had only been in the force five minutes. And wasn't Clare the one who Karen Cole had spoken to and who had found Tricky? Surely Clare deserved a chance of the attachment to CID? But Clare had done a couple of stints with CID recently, and Neil was glad not to have to work with her too closely. It irked him, though, to see someone else succeed so quickly.

Tracey drove them to Forest Fields, leaving the car in the Park and Ride scheme, along with several hundred others. A pound paid for the parking and a bus ride into the city, reducing congestion on the roads, but the two officers didn't use their free bus ride. Instead, they walked to separate ends of Hardy Street, and questioned the older women working there.

"I'm looking for someone who used to work round here," Neil said to the first woman he approached, "some time in the last five years."

"Why?" asked the peroxide blonde. "What's her speciality?"

"I wouldn't know. She's off the game now."

"Then you're wasting your time, duck," said the heavily made-up woman in the leopardskin-look leggings. "What's wrong with me, anyways?"

Neil muttered something unintelligible and backed away, embarrassed. He should be with Melanie now. Instead, it was going to be a long, uncomfortable day.

*　*　*

"Time I was getting back," Ruth told Ben late on Sunday afternoon. "Sam's cooking dinner tonight. There's probably enough for four if you want to join us."

"Better not," Ben said. "I'll come by later, pick you up."

They'd arranged to go to the pictures that evening.

"OK," Ruth told him, kissing her boyfriend gently on the cheek. "Bye." She left the flat, but instead of walking straight home, down Ebers Road, she turned into Ebers Grove, a cul-de-sac fifty yards from Ben's flat. She waited.

Three minutes later, Ben came out. He'd changed his shirt, Ruth noted. He began to walk up the hill. He would be heading for town the long way round, so that there was no risk of his passing Ruth. He would be going to see Charlene.

Not knowing what else to do, Ruth began to walk home, her eyes blurring with tears every step of the way.

15

"Oh, hi. You were here before, weren't you?"
Gary nodded.

"I hope I haven't come at a bad time."

It was Sunday afternoon and Karen had taken an age to come to the door.

"I've got a client upstairs. Can you make this quick?"

"Just one question we forgot to ask. You said something about Scott spotting a woman in the newspaper, a former prostitute who'd got married. Can you remember her name?"

"George. Short for Georgina."

"Surname?"

"I think her maiden name was Williams. I don't know the name of the bloke she married."

"Where was she living?"

"I really don't know. I haven't seen her for two, three years. Look, is there anything else?"

"A description."

"Five foot. Thin, Straight, brown hair. Plainish. I'm not very good with faces. Though…"

"What?"

Karen stared at him.

"Don't I know you from somewhere?"

"I was with PC Coppola when you spoke to her," Gary reminded her.

"No. Before that."

"Don't think so. I'd better let you get back."

"Yeah. Bye."

Gary returned to the CID office and told DI Greasby what he'd found out. Greasby checked Georgina Williams up on the Police National Computer.

"No convictions," he said. "She must've been lucky. It's going to be hard to find her."

"Isn't there some kind of computerized list of marriages?"

"No such luck. If you knew where she got married, you might have a chance. Otherwise, there's only one thing for it."

"What?"

"Get over to the Evening Post offices on Forman Street. They should have a skeleton staff on today. Go through old copies of the paper until you find the wedding photo."

Gary groaned.

"How far back should I go?"

"Start with the last six months."

"Does this mean I'm on attachment to CID?" he asked the inspector.

"Let's see if you get a result, first. But you could be useful this week, in more ways than one. I'll call Paul Grace in the morning, see how he feels about it."

"Hello, stranger, how are you?"

"Knackered. It's good to see you, though."

"You're right. It's been too long."

Neil sat down and Jan put a can of cold beer in his hand.

"No Kevin?"

She shook her head with a sigh.

"Cuts at the hospital. He has to work more weekend rotations now than when he was a house officer. Henry's beginning to forget who he is. Are you hungry?"

"Starved."

The original plan had been for Neil to bring round his girlfriend for an hour that afternoon. Jan was curious to meet this Melanie, who had replaced Clare Coppola and seemed to have done Neil a power of good.

Jan had been Neil's mentor, or tutor officer, when he was in training, and they had become friends.

Since Neil's transfer to CID they had made an effort to keep in touch.

"I'll put the microwave on."

Earlier, Neil had rung to say that he'd had to go into work, so Melanie had gone home. Jan told him to come round when he was through anyway. She'd make him some dinner. The truth was, she could do with the company.

"How's Henry?"

"He's fine. I've just got him down. How's your mum?"

"Complaining that she hasn't met Melanie yet. I'm trying to keep them apart for as long as possible, but Melanie's parents are practically demanding that I visit on my next free weekend."

"They can't be that bad if they produced her, can they?"

Neil shrugged.

"I know, but who needs it? I mean, Clare's parents, over the last two years, they practically became family. But now I don't see Nick and Maria at all. It's as if they'd died, or something. I think there should be a law against meeting your other half's parents until you're engaged, at the very least."

With Kevin's parents, Jan thought but didn't say, she'd have been happy to wait for ever.

"That's on the cards, is it," she teased Neil, "getting engaged?"

Neil looked embarrassed.

"God, no. It didn't sound like I was … sorry. It's been a long day."

"Tell me about it."

Neil filled her in on what they'd found out about Scott Travis.

"He was blackmailing a policeman – what over?"

"Probably one of two things," Neil told her. "Either it's someone who's cheating on his wife, or a closet homosexual."

"Any suspects?" Jan asked.

"Oh, it could be anyone. I've ruled out you, me, Tracey, Ruth and Clare."

"How many does that leave?"

"Fifty-something, at the minimum. Do you know anyone who's got something to hide?"

Jan thought. The only person who she suspected of playing away at the moment was Ben Shipman. Ben was one of Neil's closest friends. She couldn't tell Neil about him. Anyway, it was ridiculous. No one would murder to conceal an infidelity, not these days. And never Ben: Ben was the least violent male officer she knew.

"You do, don't you?" Neil said.

She'd delayed answering for too long.

"I guess everybody's got something to hide," Jan told him.

"I don't," Neil said. "What you see is what you get."

"Same here," Jan said. "I guess what I mean is..."

The microwave began to ping, getting her out of the conversation. Jan put plates on the table and they sat down to eat.

It was nearly six before Gary found the photo. Georgina Williams had got married in February, to a Paul Drew. A photo showed the smiling, and possibly pregnant, bride wearing white at a wedding in Wollaton village. Gary looked in the phone book. The address was there. Scott Travis probably found it the same way. That was presuming Tricky was telling the truth and Scott was blackmailing George. Gary would have to wait until tomorrow to find out. He called in, then went home to the Y.

Charlene's new flat was a set of compact, clean white rooms, sparsely decorated. She hardly seemed to live in them. Behind the roman blinds and expensive security system, it felt more like a stage set. Ben had promised himself not to come here again, yet this was his second visit of the week. He must be crazy.

Charlene looked immaculate. She was wearing a white shift which emphasized the full flow of her body. She smelt like she'd just stepped out of the shower. The next smell to hit Ben's nostrils as he sat down was Costa Rican coffee, freshly brewed, wafting from the kitchenette. Ben spoke sternly.

"I can't stay long. I told you to stop ringing me.

Why did you call?"

"I said you'd be back," Charlene told him, crossing her long legs as she sat down. "You didn't believe me, did you?"

"Look," Ben asserted himself, "I never said I wouldn't see you. I just think we need to cool it, build our separate lives. That's all."

Charlene leant forward and poured the coffee. Her neck still showed the scar where she had been cut as she jumped through the window of a burning building. It had taken her longer to return to work than the doctors expected. Maybe, she'd hinted, her injuries were more than physical. At one time Ben had thought, hoped, that his ex-girlfriend would not return to Nottingham. There was nothing here for her after all, other than work. She could pack in her job at Jagger and Co. and return to London, well out of his way.

But that hadn't happened. Jagger and Co.'s refurbished offices were officially opened last Monday, and Charlene had been there for the gala bash. He'd seen her photo in the paper. Again. Ben was convinced that the only reason Jagger had hired Charlene was because a beautiful black face was good for public relations.

Ben couldn't help caring for Charlene. You didn't go out with someone for five years and suddenly stop caring just because you'd split up. She rang to say when she was returning to Nottingham and he'd visited that night. She'd made it clear, then, that she still wanted him. And, he had to admit, he'd been tempted to go to bed with her. The attraction was still there, for both of them. He hadn't left till late. If he'd stayed any longer, he would have spent the night. Later that week, they'd argued on the phone. He'd been back, briefly, on Wednesday, to check how she was coping: very well, as it turned out.

Today there'd been another phone call, when he was with Ruth. Before Ben had hung up, claiming a wrong number, Charlene blurted out that there was something urgent she needed to discuss with him.

"Well," Ben said, sipping his coffee, which was perfect. "What is it?" Charlene lit a cigarette, fouling the air. It had been years since he'd seen her smoke. Charlene used to have the occasional cigarette at university, but only when she was under a lot of pressure.

"It concerns Jagger," she told Ben, "and your ideas about him."

Ben had tried to persuade Charlene not to work for Ian Jagger. Ben knew, but couldn't prove, that the solicitor was corrupt.

"What?"

Charlene hesitated. She finished her cigarette in long, drawn-out drags, burning off a centimetre at a time, doing God-knew-what to her fire-damaged lungs.

"I'm beginning to think that you might have been

right," she said, stubbing the butt end out in an elegant ashtray. "When you told me what Ian, I mean *Jagger*, was like, I thought you were only saying it to put me off, because you didn't want me in Nottingham."

"That's not true," Ben told her.

"Now I'm not so sure," Charlene continued, ignoring his remark. "There've been a couple of things preying on my mind."

"Like what?"

"The fire, for a start. Ian says that my getting involved in it was coincidence. I don't believe him."

She was right not to. Jagger had deliberately fed Charlene information which confused the issues in the Phoenix case. But, again, Ben couldn't prove it.

"What else?"

"Yesterday, he took me out to lunch."

"On a Saturday?" Ben said sarcastically. "That's nice for you."

"He wanted to see how I was doing," Charlene murmured. "He knows that we've split up and I'm alone. I thought it was a nice gesture. And he's easy to talk to..."

"Really?" Ben said, more sarcasm in his voice.

If she was trying to make him jealous, she was wasting her time. Jagger? Working for him was one thing, but socializing with him, for pleasure? She must be mad.

"He asked me if I still saw you, and I said

'occasionally'. Then he asked me if you were involved in the murder case which was on the news this week. I said I didn't know and asked him to tell me about the case. He said that it was about a young blackmailer who got beaten to death."

"*Blackmailer?*" Ben said. "That's the first time I've heard anyone use that word about the Scott Travis case."

"I thought that blackmail hadn't been mentioned in the papers," Charlene said, "but I wasn't sure. Before I could ask him any more about it, he changed the subject. And I wondered: *what has he got to hide?*"

"I see."

"I knew you'd want to know about it," Charlene went on. "I'm sorry I called when … she was there. I didn't know when it was best to ring."

"It's all right," Ben told her. Thankfully, Ruth didn't seem to have guessed anything. "I'll check this blackmail thing out, see if there's anything in it. In the meantime, let me know if you find out anything else."

He got up to go. Charlene leant forward for him to kiss her cold cheek. She obviously wasn't going to get up. He didn't like this frosty distance between them, but he was the one who'd chosen it. He couldn't complain. Ben saw himself to the door.

What was going on? Ben walked and walked, thinking about Charlene, thinking about Jagger, and why it was that he should let himself get mixed up with the two of them again. Why couldn't he let Charlene go completely? This evening, she'd given him a snippet of information about Jagger. But it could be that she was exaggerating, even making things up, to keep Ben's interest in her alive. Ben wasn't sure he really knew Charlene any more. Yet she still fascinated him.

Ben walked fast, towards the edge of the city. It was early evening and the traffic had slowed right down, making the fumes in the air more bearable. Jagger was sure to have lots of things to hide. What if Scott had found out one of them? From the little Ben knew about the case, the boy was too stupid, too inexperienced, to be able to blackmail someone like Jagger. But he still might have tried ... and whatever he knew could have been enough to get him killed.

Why had the solicitor mentioned the case to Charlene? Ben tried to convince himself that there was nothing to it. Scott's death was probably a drug-related murder. The idea of him being a black-mailer was just too far fetched. Still, he ought to talk to somebody about it. He ought to talk to Neil. He stopped at a phone box and dialled his friend's number. There was no one home.

Unconscious of where he'd been walking, Ben found himself out on the ring road, on the edge of Hyson Green. There was a drive-through

MacDonald's. Ben walked in and bought himself a burger and fries. He hated junk food, but nowhere else would be open, and he ought to have eaten before he went round to Ruth's.

He got to his girlfriend's house at seven-thirty, in perfect time to go out for the movie. Clare was washing up the meal plates. Ben said "hi" to her as he waited for Ruth to get changed.

"Did you hear what Clare did last night?" Ruth asked, when she came down. "No, I can see she's being too modest to tell you."

"What?"

Clare did look pretty pleased with herself, Ben noticed.

"Clare only tracked down a vital witness and worked out the motive in the Scott Travis murder. Tell him, Clare."

Clare turned from the sink to look at him, her fingers dripping.

"It turns out," she said, "that Scott Travis was an apprentice blackmailer."

16

The video was clumsily shot from street level. It showed a street of semi-detached houses, which could be one of a thousand in the city. A first-floor room had its curtains closed. As the front door opened, the picture jerked downwards and zoomed in. There was a brief glimpse of the face of a white woman, with long, dark hair. Then you saw a man coming out. He was white, with short, brown hair, and looked about forty. He was pulling on a black leather jacket. He hurried out of the house without kissing the woman goodbye, keeping his head down. Then he got into a car and drove off. Upstairs, the curtains were opened and you got a better glimpse of the woman, who was wearing a dressing gown.

The time code in the bottom right corner of the

screen indicated that the video had been taken two months ago, at one in the afternoon.

"A little lunchtime nookie," Keith Jones commented.

"Looks like it," DI Greasby said. "We don't know for sure who's being blackmailed, the woman or the man. Unfortunately, Scott Travis chose the wrong angle to get the man's numberplates, so all we know is that he drives a red Ford Sierra. We'll be circulating enhanced photos of the man and woman as soon as we get them from the lab. Any questions?"

No one spoke. Greasby continued.

"As of today, I'm adding two more people to the Scott Travis team: Keith and Gary here, who's on attachment from West. These are the areas I want you to cover: Neil and Tracey – we need to find the bloke in the video; Chris and Gary, I want you to track down the prostitute who Scott was blackmailing. Keith and I will work whatever other angles we can come up with."

"Like the identity of the policeman Scott was trying to blackmail?" Neil suggested.

"We'll look into that," Greasby said, "but I suspect it may be a blind alley. Now let's get on with it."

Gary drove to Wollaton with Chris Dylan.

"How are we going to handle this?" he asked. "I mean, if we're right and Scott Travis was blackmailing this woman, it must be because her husband doesn't know she used to be a prostitute."

"We'd better hope the husband's at work," Dylan said. "If he isn't, we'll have to find an excuse to bring the woman in, interview her separately."

Georgina Drew opened the door at nine twenty-five. She was still wearing a nightdress, maternity sized, with a cardigan around her shoulders.

"Yes?"

Georgina was heavily pregnant and looked drained. Dylan told her who he and Gary were.

"Are you alone, Mrs Drew?"

"Yes."

"Then may we come in?"

She showed them into the living room, where they sat down on red, imitation leather armchairs. Georgina excused herself and went upstairs.

"She doesn't seem too surprised to see us," Dylan commented.

They heard the toilet flush. When Georgina returned, she was wearing a dressing gown.

"Do you know what this is about?" Dylan asked.

"Not at all, no."

"You are the former Georgina Williams, known to friends as George?"

The woman's face changed and her voice became more tentative.

"Yes."

"You used to work in the Hyson Green area as a prostitute…"

"I was never convicted," George interrupted, anxiously. "I've tried to put all that behind me."

"But you couldn't, could you?" Dylan said. "Somebody wouldn't let you." Her face, already pale, became paler.

"Do you know who we're talking about?" Gary asked, gently.

She burst into tears.

"You mean Scott," she said, between sobs. "I wondered how long it would take for you to find me. I feel awful about it, awful."

"Why?" Gary asked.

She didn't reply. For a moment, Gary thought that they might be able to get a confession.

"Scott was blackmailing you," Dylan prompted.

"Scott was soft in the head," George told them. "I was sorry for him, so I gave him money. You can call it blackmail if you like, but it was like he was playing a game. Only the game was getting out of hand, so I told him it would have to stop. That's why I felt so awful."

"I don't understand," Gary said. "Why?"

"Because, last time I saw him, I told Scott if he wouldn't leave me alone, I was going to get somebody to kill him."

"This is pointless."

Neil and Tracey were driving from street to street, seeing if they could identify the house in

Scott Travis's videotape. They were still waiting for the enhanced photos of the man and woman, but had watched the tape itself ten times. There were certain details by which they could identify the house. Next door had a window box. The front gate had a slightly unusual design. There was a quite distinctive-looking bush in the small front garden. Unfortunately, Scott's camera hadn't picked up the number on the front door. Maybe the lab boys would be able to enhance that, too.

Neil's pager went off as they were turning down a sidestreet in an indeterminable area between New Basford and Sherwood. He stopped outside a house with a windowbox and read the message off it.

Please contact PCs Clare Coppola and Ben Shipman on call sign TF157. They may have important information.

Neil swore.

"What is it?" Tracey asked.

Neil told her about Saturday night.

"...it seems like she keeps muscling in on this case," he finished.

"It sounds like she's already found our two most important witnesses," Tracey corrected him. "Be grateful. We're the ones who'll end up with the credit."

Ben and Clare were waiting on the main road out-side Oxclose Lane station. There was no more room in the car park. To Neil's surprise, Clare waited in the squad car while Ben got into the back seat of Neil and Tracey's car.

"We could go inside," Neil suggested.

"Better not," Ben told him. "I'd rather Clare didn't hear this. I told her that we had to discuss personal business of yours."

"Thanks very much," Neil told him.

"Perhaps you'd like me to get out of the car, too?" Tracey suggested.

"It's all right," Ben said. "Thing is, I saw Charlene yesterday."

Ah, thought Neil. So all that's starting up again.

"She had lunch with Ian Jagger on Saturday."

Neil explained to Tracey. "Ben's ex-girlfriend is a partner at Jagger and Co. Ian Jagger is…"

"I know who Ian Jagger is."

Ben continued.

"The thing is, according to Charly … Charlene, Jagger was pumping her about the Scott Travis case, asking if I'd mentioned it to her."

"So what?" Tracey said.

Neil thought the same thing.

"So, this was on Saturday, right? Before Clare found out that Scott was into blackmail. But Jagger already knew. He more or less said that the motive for the murder was that Scott had been blackmailing the killer."

Neil and Tracey looked at one another. The solicitor's behaviour seemed bizarre. Why would he tell Charlene something like that?

"If we saw Jagger about it," Neil said, "he'd be bound to deny saying anything. It all sounds too suspicious."

"It is suspicious," Ben said. "I can't understand why he mentioned it to her. I wasn't there. Maybe he'd drunk too much and let it slip. But, if I were you, I'd try and find out if there's any connection between Jagger and Scott Travis. I'd also dig around, see if Jagger has anything to hide."

He opened the car door.

"I'll get back to you," Neil said. "Thanks, mate."

Tracey started the engine.

"What do you think?" Neil asked her.

"We're meeting the boss at two. It can wait till then."

"Fine. But what do you think about the story?"

"You're asking if I think Scott Travis could have been killed by some bigshot solicitor? I doubt it. This girl – Charlene, was it?"

"Charlene Harris."

"She's PC Shipman's bit on the side. Am I right?"

"Kind of."

Tracey smiled knowingly.

"Best bet is she's making the story up, trying to keep him interested in her. Maybe she's trying to make him jealous of her boss. She got lucky with the blackmail detail, that's all."

"You could be right," Neil had to admit.

"I think we ought to be careful how we use it," Tracey said. "Very careful indeed."

17

Ruth began her shift at two on Monday afternoon. For a few days, she and Ben had been in sync, working the same hours and both off all weekend. It had been bliss, but it wouldn't happen again for three weeks, at least. For the next few days, he had all afternoon and most of the evening to see Charlene, if that was what he wanted. What should she do about it?

Ruth's partner on patrol today was Mike Bingley. Mike wasn't Ruth's favourite person on the shift. He was a family man whose wife evidently fed him well. Only in his mid-thirties, he already had a weight problem. He didn't like having to go on the beat. Mike was one of those officers who was always going for promotion, but kept missing out. At his age, he must know that he was never likely to make sergeant. Nor was he a candidate for Traffic, or CID. She wouldn't blame him if he put less effort into the job.

Mike was holding out the colour photocopy which had been handed to them at the beginning of the shift.

"That bloke there," he said to Ruth. "What do you reckon?"

Ruth checked the man coming out of the news-agents against the fuzzy photograph.

"Could be," she said.

The man went into Grocer Jack's, came back out munching a samosa. The leather jacket he was wearing looked like the one in the photo. It was hard to be sure. His hair was a different length, but the video the photo was taken from had been shot two months before. Hair grew. Hair got cut.

"Think we should go and have a word?" Ruth said to Mike.

"Let's wait and see if he gets into that red Sierra."

The man pointed his key ring at one of the cars parked on the busy main road and deactivated the alarm. They still couldn't tell which car it was. The man walked out on to the Mansfield Road and unlocked the driver's door of the red Sierra which they had been observing.

"Bingo!" Mike said.

The Sierra set off. They wouldn't be able to stop

him now, but it didn't matter. Ruth wrote down the car's registration number.

"*Ian Jagger!* You're joking, aren't you?"

Neil tried to protest. "It was just a…"

Greasby wouldn't let him finish. "I know Jagger from the Rotary Club. A very generous guy. Does a lot for charity. He's extremely well connected. We don't offend people like him unless there's a very good reason."

"I understand. But…"

Greasby stood up. He was through with the subject.

"You'll need to get much more before I let you go anywhere near him. Now, how far have you got on the couple in the video? That's what I put you on."

"Nowhere," Neil admitted. "Tracey and I've been driving round, starting with places within walking distance of Scott's squat."

"All the beat officers should have copies by now. Maybe we'll get lucky."

"Are you putting the photos in the papers?" Neil asked.

Greasby laughed.

"And how would we phrase the appeal? *Do you know these two adulterers?* I don't think so."

Neil saw his point. The inspector's door flew open.

"*Knock* before you come in here!" Greasby ordered.

"Sorry, sir." It was Tracey. "We've just had a report. A beat officer's spotted the bloke in the video. They've got the number of his Sierra. I've got the name off the computer: Ian Lord. Address in Sherwood."

"Then you'd better get after him," Greasby said.

He looked at Neil condescendingly.

"I think we're much more likely to get a result this way. Don't you?"

Blackmail is a tricky crime to investigate, Gary decided. You can only confirm your facts by asking questions which would give the game away. They'd spent several hours interviewing Georgina Drew and got little further than they had in the first five minutes. She had done nothing to follow through her threats, she said. She wasn't serious and, anyway, Scott hadn't been back for more. Then she'd read about what had happened to him.

They needed to talk to Paul Drew. Problem was, if they let Georgina's husband know that she used to be a prostitute, they could end her marriage. Even if the husband turned out to be a very liberal guy who stuck by his wife, he would never trust her the same way again. They would have finished the blackmailer's job for him.

But what if it was Georgina who finished off the blackmailer?

And there was a further complication. Paul Drew

was George's alibi for the night of the murder. George was heavily pregnant. She said she was always fast asleep by ten, which was the earliest time that the murder could have been committed. Her husband was almost certain to confirm that alibi. But, by George's own admission, she had threatened to get someone else to kill Scott. This made an alibi meaningless. She hadn't meant it, she kept repeating. She'd only told Scott that in order to make him realize how strongly she felt. Nevertheless, she *had* said it.

Gary and Chris discussed the case in the car.

"The fact that she was so open about it must mean that she's innocent," Gary argued. "I mean, she handed us motive and method. Would a guilty person do that?"

"A stupid one might," Dylan told him. "And don't forget, she's pregnant."

"So what?"

"I remember what it was like with my ex-wife. Their hormones go crazy. Pregnant women are capable of anything except rational thought. This guy, Travis, he threatened her nest, the stability of her marriage. And she knows Nottingham. She knows people who'll beat someone senseless for the price of a vial of crack. Maybe that's what happened. The beating turned into murder, which is why she's feeling guilty."

"Maybe."

Gary found it hard to believe. George had described to them how she got herself off the streets. She went on the game at fifteen. Her pimp regularly beat her up. At seventeen, she'd gone into a hostel for battered women. While staying there, she'd come off drugs and worked as a volunteer at a shelter for the homeless. This led to a part-time, then a full-time job.

George met her husband-to-be at a Union meeting. He was a nurse at a home for the elderly. After two months, she'd moved in with him. A month later, she'd become pregnant, and he'd asked her to marry him. George always meant to tell Paul about her past, she said, but their relationship happened so quickly. She didn't want to spoil everything. A week after the marriage she'd got a phone call from Scott. At first she thought it was a joke, but she'd agreed to meet him. He had had money off her on three occasions, the last just over a fortnight ago.

"I don't see where we go from here," Gary said.

"There's only one thing to do," Chris told him. "Interview the husband."

"That's not on," Gary insisted. "She's probably innocent. It'd kill the marriage."

"That's her problem," Dylan said.

Does the job have to make you so callous? Gary wondered.

"At least we ought to let George Drew know," he suggested, "let her tell him the truth about her past first."

"And give them the chance to get their stories straight?"

They were close to the station, where they would report back to Greasby. Maybe the inspector would adopt a more caring attitude, Gary hoped. Georgina deserved the opportunity to remake her life.

They were coming off the ring road when a call came in on the radio, asking for their location. Dylan gave it.

"Look out for a red Sierra, registration Golf Two Seven Eight, Tango Vera Foxtrot, last seen heading towards Sherwood. Driver is a middle-aged white male, wanted for questioning in connection with the Scott Travis murder."

"There's a red Sierra over there," Gary pointed out.

It was coming towards them in the opposite lane.

"Call it in," Dylan ordered.

Dylan pulled a plastic cone out of the dashboard, then reached out of the window and attached the flashing blue light to the roof of the car. They accelerated to a roundabout, turned back on themselves and set off in pursuit of the Sierra.

The red car was in the fast lane of the dual carriageway. Dylan closed on it. At the next roundabout, another unmarked CID car joined the chase. Gary could see Neil Foster in the driving seat. The driver of the red Sierra, however, was oblivious to the cars following him.

They were passing the Whitemoor Estate. There were plenty of side roads which the officers could force the Sierra to turn into. But the guy was still in the fast lane. Gary watched as Neil drove alongside him and tried to gesture the driver to pull over. He didn't seem to notice.

"Maybe it'd be easier to keep following him," Gary suggested. "See where he ends up."

"And suppose he's on a jaunt to London?" Dylan retorted.

Ahead of them, the Sierra signalled right. There were gaps in the central reservation of the dual carriageway which allowed cars to turn right. The Sierra pulled into one of them. Dylan braked sharply behind it, blocking the fast lane. Behind Dylan, car horns were sounded as he forced the traffic behind him to swerve into the inside lane. On the road ahead, Gary could see Neil and Tracey, turning into the next gap in the road, ready to double back on themselves.

The red Sierra found a brief gap in the traffic. It hurtled across both lanes of the carriageway into a side street, causing cars to brake and nearly collide. There was no way for Dylan to follow immediately. Somehow, Neil and Tracey managed to cut across the road, swerve through the traffic and follow the Sierra into the side street. Thirty seconds later, Gary and Dylan went after them.

The man who got out of the car looked at Neil

and Tracey, who had parked ahead of him, then at Gary and Chris, who were in the process of parking behind him.

"Are you following me?" he asked.

Neil almost felt like laughing.

"Ian Lord?" he asked.

"That's me."

Neil held out his warrant card.

"DC Foster, CID. We'd like to ask you a few questions."

"What's going on?"

A woman in a blue housecoat had come out of a house a few doors down the road. Neil recognized her. She was in the video. And so was the house that she had come out of. There was the gate, the bush, the window box. He turned to the other three. Excited glances showed that they had all noticed the same thing.

"I think we'd better interview these two separately," he suggested.

Dylan nodded.

"Four of you?" Ian Lord said. "What is this? All right, I know I was speeding, but, four of you...?"

Neil put on his most diplomatic voice.

"If you wouldn't mind getting into the car, sir?"

Ian Lord gave his female friend an exasperated look.

"I've no idea what's going on, Pauline."

"What is this?" The woman he'd just called

Pauline said, as her lover let Tracey guide him into the back seat of the police car. Neil spoke to her.

"Perhaps we could have a word with you, too, Mrs…?"

"Jones. Pauline Jones. What is this about?"

"It's be better if we talked inside. Your neighbours…"

"Yes, yes."

"We'll just be a moment," Neil told her, then turned to consult Dylan.

"You and Tracey take the woman," the sergeant said. "We'll take the bloke."

"Here?" Neil asked.

"No, let's have them both back at the station. I'll call in, make sure there are two interview rooms free."

A minute later, Neil and Tracey were inside the house they'd been looking for all morning.

"It's a sensitive matter," Neil told Pauline Jones. "I'm afraid I need to ask you to accompany me to the station."

"My husband'll be home in a couple of hours."

"We'll try and have you back by then."

Mrs Jones screwed her eyes up, trying to make sense of what was happening. She had been expecting a visit from her lover and the police had turned up instead. But adultery wasn't against the law, not in this country, anyhow. She looked at Neil and he smiled back with what he hoped looked like sympathy.

"You'll at least allow me to get dressed?" she said.

"Of course," Tracey told her. "You don't mind if I come with you, do you?"

"Why on earth would you want to do that?"

She might try to hide or destroy evidence, that was why.

"Normal procedure," Tracey assured her.

Pauline Jones' stare became hard now, brass-faced. Reluctantly, she let Tracey follow her upstairs.

18

It took most of Monday for Charlene to get Jagger on his own. Hearing him put down the phone, she tapped on his door, poked her head inside his office, and asked if he'd got a minute. Ian Jagger gave his benign smile, said *of course*, then patiently answered her imaginary query about a custody hearing.

"That's given you a lot of headaches, hasn't it?" her boss finished, with a kindly smile. When Charlene began to work for the solicitor, she'd thought of him as a bit of an old buffer, with his greying hair and old-fashioned mannerisms. But, as she'd got to know him, it became clear that Ian Jagger had the energy of a man half his age. She would never underestimate his experience, or his power.

"I think I'm on top of it now," Charlene told him, then added, "Actually, there was one other thing I wanted to know."

"Always willing to help."

Charlene tried to sound casual.

"At lunch on Saturday, you asked about that boy who was killed – Scott something?"

"Did I?" He smiled, acting forgetful.

"Only, you set me thinking," she continued. "Why do you think that this Scott boy was a blackmailer?"

Jagger scratched his chin and gave her a long, analytical look.

"You hear many things in this office that are confidential," he said.

"Yes, and I always keep those confidences," Charlene said, firmly, "but colleagues share most things, don't they?"

"Quite. Tell me, under what circumstances does the law allow you to break a confidence?"

"Parts of the Children Act attempt to override client/lawyer privilege, in cases of child abuse, and similar areas."

Jagger nodded. He did this sometimes, acting like they were in a university tutorial.

"Still, most of our profession disagree with those provisions in the act, and they're virtually impossible to enforce."

"Virtually."

They were poker players now, facing each other down. Charlene had to decide whether to call the other solicitor's bluff.

"Who was Scott Travis blackmailing?" she asked.

"More than one person, probably," Jagger told her. "Most blackmailers do. Although I gather that Mr Travis wasn't a very competent blackmailer."

"You seem to know a lot about him," Charlene commented.

"Yes," Jagger said. "And I'm sure you can guess how. But I was being indiscreet over a very pleasant lunch. I shouldn't have told you so much. You'll forgive me if I close the subject?"

Now he was calling her bluff. Did Jagger know the identity of the murderer? Was it possible that he... Charlene couldn't think of a subtle enough way to phrase the question.

"Just curious," she said.

"A useful trait, in its place. Seen anything of your ex-boyfriend lately?"

Charlene blushed.

"Never mind," Jagger said. "I was just curious."

The three detectives and Gary sat in the CID room, waiting for Greasby to join them so that they could work out a game plan for the interviews.

"Did she say anything in the car?" Dylan asked.

"Not a dicky bird," Neil told him. "Yours?"

"Said he'd been knocking her off for six months,"

Dylan announced. "Told us he was seeing this bird in Mansfield, too. He gets around, repairs TVs, videos. Great way to meet women, he told us."

It wasn't a crime last time I heard, was what he'd said, *unless the wife finds out, that is.*

The phone rang. Dylan answered it.

"Yeah. All right. Yeah. I'll let you know."

He put the phone down again.

"The DI's delayed. We're to do this on our own. Tracey, try and soften her up a bit first. Don't mention blackmail unless she brings it up. Show her the photo of Travis but don't mention his name. See if she knows it. All right?" Tracey assented. She and Neil went off to interview room one. Dylan turned to Gary.

"All right, new boy. Time to listen and learn."

He followed the DS to interview room two.

"Now will you tell me what this is about?"

Ian Lord sounded exasperated.

"All in good time," Dylan told him.

The mobile phone in the repairman's pocket began to ring.

"May I?" he asked.

"Make it quick," Dylan told him. "Then switch it off."

They listened while Lord told a customer that he'd be delayed. As he was putting the phone away, Dylan put a photograph of Scott Travis on to the table between them.

"Ever seen this young man before?" he asked.

Ian Lord examined it closely.

"I don't think so. Should I have?"

His face was blank.

"Maybe," Dylan said. "Take a closer look."

"Has he been in the newspapers? Yes. That's it. *Evening Post*, last week: *the police request any inform-ation about*... This is some poor homeless lad who got himself murdered. Why are you asking me about him?"

"Perhaps you could tell us," Dylan said, "where you were on the night of Monday last, from ten onwards."

"Oh, come on," Ian Lord said. "You can't seriously think that I had anything to do with that lad's death, can you?"

"Try us and see."

"You said this'd be quick. My husband gets home in just over an hour."

"We'll be as quick as we can," Tracey assured Pauline Jones. "How long it takes depends on you. Now, I think that you know what this is all about..."

"I haven't the slightest idea," Pauline Jones protested.

She looked guilty, Neil thought. But if he'd been caught committing adultery, he might look the same.

"I think you do," Tracey told her. "Have you told Ian about it?"

"Told him what?"

"About the trouble your little affair's got the two of you into."

Neil admired Tracey's gambit. What the police didn't know was whether Scott had been blackmailing one, or both of the couple. And, if it was one of them, had that one told the other? Mrs Jones wasn't playing along.

"My husband has no idea," Pauline said, "if that's what you're getting at. And I've no intention of him finding out. He's a cook at the Royal Hotel in town. He works really long hours. So, you know, I get lonely. Not that it's any business of yours."

"And who else knows about your relationship with Ian, Pauline?" This time, Neil thought he saw a flicker of guilt cross Pauline's brow.

"No one."

"You haven't told a friend?"

She shook her head. Tracey's voice became lower, insinuating.

"But people always notice, don't they? A neighbour…"

"Ian always parks a bit down the street. He brings in his tool kit. It's not like we're at it every day. Once a fortnight, he comes round. Once a week if I'm lucky."

"But someone's noticed, haven't they?"

"I've told you…"

Tracey looked at Neil, a question in her eyes. Neil

nodded. They weren't going to get any further without playing their trump card. He took the photograph of Scott Travis from his pocket.

"Do you recognize this young man, Pauline?"

She barely glanced at it, then shook her head.

"Take another look," Tracey told her.

She forced herself to.

"You know him, don't you?"

Pauline was silent.

"He sent you something, didn't he? Or maybe he hand-delivered it, during the day, when your husband was out."

"I don't know what…"

There was no energy left in her denial.

"We'll stay here all day, if necessary, Pauline. But if you tell us the truth, you could be out of here in five minutes."

Five minutes was an exaggeration, but Pauline Jones grasped the idea like a lifeline.

"All right. Yes. It's true. This boy, he sent me a video of Ian leaving my place. I met him a couple of weeks ago, gave him fifty quid. He told me that he'd return the original tape. Never did though. I'm surprised he hasn't been back for more."

"Did you tell Ian about it?" Tracey wanted to know.

"God, no. If Ian thought that his wife would find out, he'd drop me just like that. He told me if I so much as phone him at home once, it's over."

"So you paid the boy fifty pounds. How did he get in touch?"

"Phone call. He was really nervous-sounding, just a kid. When I met him, I expected him to be younger. I don't think he'd done it before. Blackmail, I mean. He seemed really embarrassed about it all."

"Where did you meet him?"

The reply surprised Neil.

"He came to the house."

"Really?" Tracey asked.

It was too much to hope that they would have met on Weston Avenue, but Scott's going to Pauline's house showed incredible nerve, or stupidity.

"I gave him the fifty quid, told him that was all he was getting, and waited for him to sod off. But he hung around, asking me questions, looking at things. He was creepy."

"And you never saw him again?" Neil asked.

"No. Not since then."

"You didn't read about him in the newspapers?"

"I don't get a newspaper."

"Not even a freesheet?"

"They come, but I throw them in the bin."

Neil and Tracey looked at each other. Either Pauline was telling the truth or she was a convincing liar.

"Is that what this is about?" she asked them. "Has this lad been caught blackmailing someone else?"

"Not exactly," Tracey said. "Can you tell us what you were doing the Monday before last between ten at night and two in the morning?"

Pauline thought for a moment.

"My husband, Jeff, he has Monday nights off. We were at the pictures. A quick drink in the Bell afterwards, then home to bed. Why?"

"Because," Tracey told her, "that's when the boy who was blackmailing you got himself murdered."

19

Ben was asleep when the phone rang.

"I'm sorry it's so early. I tried last night but you were out."

"I went for a drink with Neil," Ben told Charlene, wondering why he had to account for himself to her. "What's this about?"

"I spoke to Jagger again, like you asked me to."

Ben was rapidly waking up. Not for the first time, it occurred to him that Charlene's story about Jagger might merely be an excuse to keep seeing him. She told him about the conversation she'd had with the solicitor the previous afternoon.

"He seemed to be implying that one of his clients was being blackmailed by Scott Travis."

"Can you find out which one?" Ben wanted to know.

"I can't go sneaking through filing cabinets," Charlene said. "It wouldn't be ethical. And even if I did look, I can't see Ian keeping a written record of anything connected to blackmail."

"Is it possible that Jagger's the one who was being blackmailed?" Ben asked. "Maybe he let the word slip by accident and now he's backtracking."

"I don't know," Charlene said, sounding agitated. "You're the one who's convinced he's got a shady past."

Ben thought for a moment.

"How did his wife die?" he asked. "Did you ever find that out?"

"You don't just ask a question like that," Charlene said, tetchily.

"Wouldn't one of the other partners know?"

Charlene was hesitant.

"Maybe... I mean, I'll try to find out, but bear in mind it is possible that Ian's trying to act for the best. He wanted the police to know that this boy was a blackmailer because the investigation wouldn't get anywhere otherwise. As it happened, CID had just worked out the same thing."

"And why did he mention the Children's Act?" Ben asked.

It all smelt suspicious to him.

"I guess he had to have some excuse for breaking client confidentiality."

"Or he was deliberately confusing the issue," Ben

argued. "Be careful around him, Charlene."

"I am."

CID had hit another brick wall. Each of their suspects had alibis for the night of Scott's murder, but none of these, with the exception of Max Walker's, were cast iron. Each depended on the evidence of a spouse. Trouble was, the alibi witnesses couldn't be questioned too closely, because to do so would give the game away. Each had been told that they were being interviewed in connection with an (imaginary) crime near their home. Each had confirmed their husband or wife's story.

"Shouldn't we look into the police officer angle?" Neil suggested at their Tuesday morning meeting.

"I'm doing that," Greasby said, off-handedly. "Meanwhile, I suggest that you and Tracey try showing photos of our three main suspects around Weston Avenue. If someone recognizes one of them, we could get lucky."

Before Neil could go out, there was a phone call from Ben. He listened incredulously as Ben laid out a theory about Ian Jagger's late wife. Neil promised to check out how the woman had died. After all, they'd been told to lay off Jagger, not his wife. And, anyway, she wasn't alive to complain. He made a couple of phone calls and discovered that the woman was called Pamela. She'd died in a car crash. He asked to be sent the autopsy report.

"Ready?" Tracey called to Neil.

"Do you mind taking someone else?" he asked her. "I've got an angle I'm looking into here."

Tracey shrugged and went to get Gary. While Neil waited for Pamela Jagger's autopsy report to be faxed to him, he thought about Melanie. When she rang last night, he'd promised to visit her and her parents this weekend. That was, if he didn't have to do more overtime on the Scott Travis case. He needed to be with Melanie, and was feeling guilty about having to desert her on Saturday. But he wasn't looking forward to meeting her parents. What would they think of him? When you sent your only daughter off to university, you expected her to bring back another student as a boyfriend, not a policeman three years older with only a handful of GCSEs to his name.

The whirr of the fax machine interrupted his thoughts. The report it brought made interesting reading. Neil didn't know Jagger, but had built up a mental picture of someone well into middle age. He expected the lawyer's wife to be of a similar vintage. Not so. Pamela Jagger, when she died, was only thirty years old, ten years younger than her husband was at the time. She was also black.

The autopsy described how Pamela's neck had been broken when she wrapped her car around a lamppost. She had slightly more than the legal limit for alcohol in her system, which may have been a contributory factor in her losing control of the car. The police notes said that there were no suspicious circumstances, although it was hard to know how she came to crash. The night of the accident there was good visibility. It was two in the morning. The roads were clear. Unfortunately, this also meant that there were no witnesses to whatever had occurred.

What if Scott Travis had been there? What if he'd seen something? Scott would have been – how old, then? – fourteen. He'd hardly started absconding from Holyleigh house at that age. It was an unlikely thesis, Neil knew. Pamela's husband, the records said, was at home in bed at the time of the crash. He could offer no explanation for his wife's being out in the early hours of the morning. She was a criminal lawyer, like himself. Sometimes, he told the police, she had to meet clients in odd places, at odd times. But they couldn't check Pamela's diary, because it had been destroyed in the fire which engulfed her car. She'd been trapped inside, and the car went up before the emergency services managed to get there.

Neil found himself feeling sorry for the lawyer. What a terrible way to lose someone. Unless … unless he was responsible for her death.

"I don't think it's any of them," Tracey told Neil, later in the day, as they drove back to the White-moor estate to reinterview Pauline Jones. "Think about it. None of these people had enough to lose.

It's worth fifty quid to Pauline for her husband not to find out, sure. But … a *life*? I don't think so."

"The bloke – Ian Lord? According to Pauline, he was really concerned about his wife finding out."

Tracey sneered.

"That's his way of making sure that Pauline keeps her distance, doesn't become a problem. You heard how he boasted about having two mistresses on the go. If he's really a philanderer, his wife's bound to know. She puts up with it."

Tracey was making sense, Neil thought.

"Georgina Drew had the most to lose," he said.

"Yes, but she can't have done it herself – she wasn't physically capable. So where does that leave us – that she paid some lowlife to *execute* Scott? I don't think so. This is Nottingham, not Chicago in the twenties."

Neil laughed.

"So who do you reckon did it?" he asked.

Tracey pulled up outside Pauline Jones's council semi.

"Someone we haven't got to yet," she said. "Someone who has a lot to lose."

"Like who?" Neil asked.

"Someone in a position of power. Your lawyer's a possibility, but he's too clever. He wouldn't have done it himself."

"Maybe. Maybe not."

You never knew with crimes of violence, Neil

thought. Some people suddenly cracked. The most unlikely people, too. Tracey carried on.

"I think that the angle we've ignored is the policeman. Scott was connected to the gay scene. He went to clubs with Karen Cole. I reckon we're looking for a gay policeman with some kinky habits and good connections."

"Why good connections?" Neil asked.

"Look at the way the DI's steering us away from looking at the police angle on the murder. Someone's warned him off."

"Perhaps you think it's Greasby himself," Neil teased.

He couldn't take the whole idea seriously.

"No," Tracey said. "It's a uniform."

"Why?"

"Look at the way Scott was killed – a heavy, blunt object. What does it sound like to you?"

"A truncheon," he said.

"Precisely," Tracey told him. "Gay cop. Uniform. Position of some power. Any ideas?"

Inspector Grace, Neil thought, but didn't say aloud.

"I'll pick you up at seven," Paul Grace told Clare as her shift ended at two that afternoon. "Probably in a taxi."

"I thought you didn't drink," Clare said, confused by the taxi.

"I never touch the stuff when I'm driving, but tomorrow night I might need some Dutch courage."

"In that case," Clare suggested, "what's the point of paying extra for a taxi back into the city? You live in Arnold. It's on my way."

"I ... uh."

"Give me your address. I'll book a taxi and pick you up at seven-twenty. Does that sound all right?"

"Very sensible," Grace told her. "It's just that I like to be – what's the word? Chivalrous."

"You're in the wrong century," Clare told him. "We're both doing this for our careers, remember? You seem more nervous about it than I do."

Grace gave her a funny look.

"Maybe I've got more to lose," he said, then wrote down his address.

"How long do these things normally go on?" Clare asked him.

"To be honest, I've no idea. No later than one, I'd have thought."

Jan came in. Clare still hadn't told her that she was going out with Grace at the weekend. She had a feeling that Jan, for whatever reason, wouldn't approve.

"Any idea when we're getting Gary back?" the sergeant asked the inspector. Grace gave her an apologetic smile.

"I'll give DI Greasby a call, if you like, tell him

we need Gary by the end of the week. If he's not back soon, we'll all have forgotten who he is." No one smiled at this weak joke.

"Clare," Jan said as she closed the door, "I'm putting you with Ben tomorrow, foot patrol. All right?"

"Fine."

Clare looked down at her feet. She'd been walking all day today as well. She hated her feet and was suddenly conscious of Grace looking at them. They were too big. They got tired too quickly. The last thing she felt like doing, most nights, was dancing.

"Want me to have a word?" Grace said, gently. "Get her to put you in a car?"

"No thanks," Clare said, politely. "I don't want any favours."

Grace nodded as if to say that she was being wise.

"See you tomorrow, Clare."

"Tomorrow."

He was a nice man, Clare decided, as she watched him leave. She wondered if he had someone to go home to. She wished that she did.

"What's going on with you and the inspector?" Jan asked, back in the parade room.

"How do you mean?"

"Come on, Clare, that must be the third 'little chat' I've seen you have with him in the last week."

"If you must know —"

Tim Cooper came in.

"I'll give you a lift home," Jan told Clare. "Henry's at his gran's today."

Once they were in Jan's green Citroën, Clare explained.

"*Mess night!*" Jan exclaimed. "It can't be one of those, not at Epperstone. And Grace wouldn't be allowed to take you, not unless you were married to him. They're wives only. It must be a mess ball."

"What's the difference?"

"They have dancing, I think. And lots of hob-nobbing. Not that I'd know. I've never been to one. I don't even know anyone who's been to one. The tickets cost a fortune."

"Any advice?" Clare asked, nervously.

"Yes. Don't go. But it's too late for that, isn't it? I thought you'd learnt your lesson about dating police officers after the way you messed Neil about."

Clare ignored the criticism.

"It's not a date, it's…"

"Paul Grace is a cold fish," Jan warned her. "He's clever, calculating. I respect him, but I don't like him. You ought to be careful, Clare."

"I will be," Clare promised.

"What are you after this time?" Pauline Jones wanted to know. She looked around to see if the neighbours were watching. They were. Tracey spoke reassuringly.

"We're calling to see if you've remembered anything else."

"I haven't."

"Can we come in anyway?" Neil asked, foot firmly inside the door.

"I suppose."

Pauline Jones looked different from the day before: no make-up, hair tied back, showing her age. She was thirty-five, Neil remembered, only a few years older than Jan, but she showed every one of them.

"Jeff suspected," she told them. "Last night, he knew something was up. I'm going to have to stop seeing Ian. I hope you're happy about that."

"It's not our job to moralize," Tracey said. "But someone's dead. We have to find out who killed him."

Pauline sighed and lit a cigarette.

"Asked for it, though, didn't he? Blackmail, that's a big boy's game. You could tell at a glance that he wasn't up to it."

"You didn't think he'd really show the tape to your husband?" Neil asked.

"I wasn't sure," Pauline said. "He gave me the feeling that the tape wasn't what it was all about. He had this look about him. He seemed … needy."

Neil began to ask a question.

"Did Scott Travis…?"

"What did you say?" Pauline Jones interrupted, her voice taking on a harsher, broad Nottingham tone. Neil looked up. There was a new anxiety in her eyes.

"I was going to ask…"

"The boy's name," Pauline interrupted again. "You started to say the boy's name. Yesterday, you never mentioned it."

"We wanted to see if you knew it," Tracey explained, patiently. "The dead boy's name was Scott Travis."

Pauline's eyes glazed. She gripped the side of the armchair, dropped her cigarette, and fainted.

While Tracey revived Pauline, Neil put the cigarette in the ashtray, went to the kitchen and poured a glass of water. It took a couple of minutes for her to come round fully.

"What is it?" Tracey asked. "Why did the mention of Scott's name affect you so?"

"Because…" Pauline said, beginning to sob now. "Because he was my son."

20

"How do I look?" Clare asked, greeting Ruth and Sam in the kitchen. The only decent black dress she owned had been bought for her brother's funeral, nearly two years before. It was tight on her, and had bad associations, so she'd spent a small fortune on a new one in Jigsaw that afternoon. Ruth reached forward and pinched her waist.

"Are you starting to put on weight?" she asked, half seriously.

Clare slapped her hand away.

"It's not too much cleavage, is it?"

"Just right," Sam assured her.

"Any more and you'll give the older officers heart attacks," Ruth joked.

"Luckily, that won't be a problem with Paul Grace."

"Are you sure you're not going to be bored to death?" Sam asked. "All those middle-aged men."

Clare shrugged.

"Paul might turn out to be good company," she said. "Out of uniform, he seems nice enough. If not, maybe I'll get lucky and there'll be a cute waiter."

"But what if both of you go after the same cute waiter?" Ruth teased.

Outside, a taxi sounded its horn.

"See you later," Clare said.

Paul Grace's house was on a modern estate full of sloping angles and bricks which didn't quite look real. The houses were all different but, in a funny way, seemed to blend into one. They reminded Clare of Duplo. She could tell which one was the inspector's by the red Mazda in the drive. She got out of the taxi to collect him, curious to get a glance inside, find out a bit more about her boss. She was five minutes early.

Grace answered the door in his shirt sleeves. He had a white dress-shirt on, its ruffles expertly ironed. The collar was turned up and he had a red band around it.

"Clare! Is it that time already? I can't get this bloody dicky-bow tied." He reminded her of her younger brother, on his first day at secondary school.

"Come on," she said. "Get in front of a mirror. I'll show you how."

There had been a hall ball in her second term at university. Karl, her then boyfriend, had worn a bow tie for a laugh, a proper one. Between them, they had worked out how to put it on.

She liked the inside of the inspector's house, what little she saw of it. There were shelves full of books, nice prints on the walls. The decor was in carefully balanced, muted colours, with discreet mood lighting. It looked like the cliché about gay men was really true. They had good taste in interior design. Clare leant over his back as she did his tie in the bathroom mirror.

"There. That's perfect. We'd better go."

Paul grabbed his jacket from the bedroom. Through the open door, Clare got a brief glance of a double bed. She wondered who he shared it with.

"I had to hire this stuff specially. Tradition, or something. Do I look a complete prat?"

Clare giggled. The blue and black jacket was rather silly. It was cut very short, like something a pageboy might wear in an old-fashioned play. Grace's dark trousers had a blue stripe down the side. It looked terribly military. She said nothing. At the door, Grace seemed to notice her for the first time.

"I must say, Clare, you look ravishing."

"Thank you," she said, getting into the taxi.

Suddenly, she found herself nervous. What in heaven's name was she thinking of, going to a do like this? But it was too late to get out of it.

"Thank you. That was a brilliant dinner," Neil told Mrs Byatt.

"Coffee?"

"We ought to be getting off to the Rose and Crown soon," Melanie said. "Tanya and Jordan are expecting us."

"I'm sure you've got time for a quick coffee," her father said. "We've hardly had any time to talk to Neil so far."

Melanie had done her bit, keeping Neil busy so that her parents didn't have the opportunity to give him a full-scale interrogation. Somehow, he had always managed to avoid this scene with his previous girlfriends. He had become close to the Coppolas, but he had been looking into the death of their son before he started dating their daughter. They already knew him, trusted him.

"And how long have you been in the police?" Louise Byatt asked.

"Two and a half years," Neil told her.

"And what did you do before that?"

"School. A couple of dead-end jobs."

"You didn't do A-levels?"

"I went to college for half a term, but I've never been academic. I knew then that I was interested in joining the force, but they don't like to take people under nineteen. So I messed around a bit, doing this and that, trying to decide if it was definitely what I wanted to do."

"Why the police?" Mrs Byatt asked.

"It sounded more interesting than most careers. And I wanted a steady job, one where they weren't too likely to make you redundant. My dad was on the dole for ten years before he died. I saw what that did to him."

The Byatts regarded Neil with a mixture of sympathy and disbelief. They looked like neither of them had seen the inside of a DSS office in their lives.

"We really ought to be going," Melanie said.

As they walked to the pub, Neil told her the latest about the Scott Travis case.

"So it turns out that this Pauline Jones was his mother. Travis is her maiden name. She had him when she was sixteen, tried to bring him up on her own but couldn't cope. He was taken into care when he was three. She met Jeff Jones a couple of years later. He wasn't interested, so she stopped seeing Scott. She thought he'd been adopted, she said, but I think she was lying, or conning herself. He became inconvenient and she dropped him from her life."

"And she didn't recognize her own son?"

"It was nearly fifteen years since she'd seen him. He acted weirdly, asking a lot of questions, looking around the house, that kind of thing. He didn't seem all that interested in the money, either, but Pauline didn't pick up on any of that. She was terrified that Scott would tell her husband about the affair. The possibility of Scott being who he was just didn't occur to her."

"So you're ruling Pauline Jones out as a suspect?" Melanie asked.

"She's pretty low down the league table at the moment."

"What about Max?" Melanie asked, as they turned down a leafy street.

"He's the only one with a cast-iron alibi, isn't he?"

"The hospital? I've been thinking about that."

They were nearly at the pub. She stopped walking.

"Have you had your tonsils out?"

"No," Neil said.

"They keep you in for two nights, minimum, but, the first night, there's nothing wrong with you. Basically, they have you there to stop you eating before the op."

"What are you saying?" Neil asked.

"All I'm saying is, it's not like you're in prison. Lights go out at nine or ten or whenever it is. It would be pretty easy for Max to sneak out, kill Scott, get rid of his clothes, then go back to his hospital bed with the perfect alibi."

Neil grinned.

"You've got a devious mind, Melanie Byatt, but that's a bit Sherlock Holmes. I thought this guy was a friend of yours."

Melanie shrugged.

"We share the same pastoral tutor, that's all. If he did kill this poor boy, I'd like you to be able to prove it."

"I'll go back to the hospital first thing Monday," Neil said. "Find out if he really could have got away. Thanks, Mel. That's really helpful."

She slipped her arm around his waist and they stopped to kiss in the street, not caring who saw them.

They'd set up a marquee outside Epperstone Manor. The guests' average age, Clare was scared to note, was at least twice her own. All of the men wore the same silly uniform as Paul. All of the women wore black dresses, most of them much more formal than hers. Everyone but her sported plenty of jewellery. Clare felt very self-conscious.

"I'm not sure I can go through with this," she told Paul as they stepped into the marquee.

"You'll be fine. Be thankful this isn't a standard Mess night. No dancing there. Umpteen courses and an after-dinner speaker. Know who the last one was?"

"No idea."

"The Right Honourable Roger Wellington, MP, our former Home Secretary."

"It's a relief not to have to hear him," Clare agreed.

Keeping Clare attached to his arm, Grace floated around the marquee. He was very nervous, she could tell, but he put on a good show, saying hello to as many people as possible, holding brief but intelligent conversations.

"You're very good at remembering names," she told him.

"You ought to work out your own technique," he told her. "The way I do it: picture the person in your head, repeat the name to yourself until it's sunk in."

"Thanks for the advice."

He looked at her to see if she was being sarcastic. Clare wasn't sure herself.

"Also," he went on, "you should try and talk more, Clare. Make an impression."

Clare knew that she was already making an impression. She had seen the way the officers' wives looked at her. She didn't want to draw any more attention to herself than she was doing already.

"I'm content to be an ornament tonight," she said.

"I never thought I'd hear you say something like that."

Clare smiled. She enjoyed shocking him.

"This isn't about either of us being ourselves, is it?"

Paul gave her a peculiar look and didn't reply. A minute later, they were on the edge of a group including the chief constable. Bad jokes were laughed at.

"And what do you do, dear?" asked the fifty-something wife of a superintendent, as Paul chatted up her husband. Clare was fed up of this question.

"I work for an escort agency."

For a moment, she thought she'd actually said the words aloud, but then she saw that the woman was still waiting for an answer.

"Oh, I'm in the police, too," she said, in her most throwaway voice. "Nothing very exciting, I'm afraid."

The superintendent's wife nodded politely. She would assume that Clare was a typist or recep-tionist. Let her. A gong sounded. Clare was very grateful that it was time to eat.

Dinner – all seven courses of it – seemed to last for ever. At least they were sat with other younger officers, and the conversation moved around fairly comfortable topics: football, concerts and clubs, together with snippets of gossip about members of the still more senior ranks. Clare kept a low profile. Afterwards, there was dancing, to a small orchestra. Clare sank into Paul Grace's arms with relief. She didn't have to make superficial conversation any more. He held her tightly.

"You've done brilliantly tonight, Clare."

"Not as well as you have."

"Thanks for coming with me. I really appreciate it."

"It's been an experience," Clare admitted. "How long do we have to stay?"

"Another hour or two. I believe the ballroom dancing gives way to disco at midnight."

"I don't know if I've got the energy for disco," Clare admitted. Her feet hurt.

"I must say," Paul told her, affectionately stroking her hair as the band played *Moon River*, "I'm very happy just doing this. Are you?"

"I am," Clare said.

They danced until the orchestra packed up and went home. The crowd had started to thin. Those left were mainly the younger senior officers and the serious drinkers. A DJ began to play bad hits from the seventies. Without a word, Paul guided Clare from the dance floor to a chair. By now, her feet were killing her. She sat down while Paul went to order a taxi.

He hadn't asked whether she wanted another drink, but came back with champagne.

"Let's go outside," he suggested.

"Sure."

Clare was already a little tipsy, and the champagne went straight to her head. Sensing her unsteadiness, Paul guided her out to a bench near the manor itself, where they could see the taxi when it arrived. The night had been warm, but it was late now and Clare's dress was thin. She shivered a little.

"Here. Let me."

Paul Grace took off his pageboy's jacket and put it around Clare's shoulders.

"Thanks," she said. "I must look ridiculous."

"No, you don't," he told her. "You look gorgeous."

Clare gave him a weak smile. She'd never been terribly good at taking a compliment. She usually thought it meant that the giver wanted something.

"It's a beautiful moon," she said, pointing at the sky.

Out of the city, you could see so many more stars. It made her feel romantic – or maybe it was only the champagne doing its work.

"I mean it," Paul Grace said. "You're beautiful."

Embarrassed, Clare avoided looking at him.

"You're drunk," she said, gently.

"No, I'm not."

He put an arm around her shoulder in an affectionate, non-threatening way. It felt good. Clare let herself lean towards him.

"This is nice," she said.

"It could be nicer."

He kissed her gently on the lips. Clare was confused. Had he ever actually told her that he…? She couldn't remember. All she knew was that he was pulling her close to him now and this kiss was a full one and there was no mistaking the way his body felt against hers.

"You're not gay," she said, when they finally broke apart.

"Pardon?"

"People thought ... I thought that you were asking me out to cover for the fact that you ... like men."

Paul held his head back and laughed. He drained his glass of champagne, then spoke to her earnestly.

"I like women, Clare, but I'm shy around them. I find it hard to tell them what to do. Jan Hunt – you mustn't tell her this – she scares me to death."

"She scares me sometimes too," Clare admitted.

"And you scare me. I've been trying to find a way to get us ... like this, ever since Neil left the shift."

"Really?"

Clare didn't know what was going on. Paul gazed intently into her eyes.

"I'm crazy about you, Clare."

"Oh, God."

Not knowing what else to do, Clare kissed him again. This time, their embrace was interrupted by a taxi horn.

"Quickly," Grace said, pulling away from her. "You know how immoral drunken policemen are. Let's run down before somebody steals it!"

Laughing, hand in hand, they ran across the green lawns for their taxi.

At one in the morning, somebody woke Neil. A warm body was pressed against his.

"Oh, Clare, sorry. Did I fall asleep?"

"I'm not Clare," Melanie said, in a cold voice.

Neil blinked fully awake. They were squashed together in a single bed: the guest bedroom of her parents' house.

"Sorry, Mel," he whispered. "I didn't know where I was for a moment."

"So I gathered."

He kissed her tenderly, hoping that he hadn't hurt her too much. Melanie began to question him.

"I thought you told me that you and she didn't, you know, do it?" There was a tentative quality to her voice which might be jealousy.

"She'd never go all the way," Neil affirmed. "She said she had to be sure. Some kind of Catholic thing, I guess."

"Most men wouldn't put up with that."

"I'm not most men."

"No. You're not," she said, kissing him on the forehead and getting out of bed. He had a brief glimpse of her beautiful body. Then she put on her dressing gown and slipped back to her room.

Clare kissed and cuddled Paul all the way back to

Arnold. The tension she'd felt earlier in the evening was gone. She couldn't remember when she last felt as sexy as this. Just after Neil moved into his house, perhaps. That night when he had asked her to marry him and she had nearly, nearly gone to bed with him for the first time.

"Not here," she said, as one of Paul Grace's hands slipped inside her dress.

"You're not a prude, are you?" Paul teased, whispering in her ear, then licking it.

"I didn't think that anyone used that word any more," Clare told him.

"You'll have to excuse me. I went to a public school."

Clare laughed.

"I try to keep that quiet," Paul added.

"You're wasting your time," Clare told him. "We all guessed."

They both burst into a fit of the giggles again.

"I wish we had some more champagne," Clare said.

Paul whispered in her ear.

"We're nearly home. There's a bottle in my fridge. We can take it to bed." He kissed her again, even more passionately this time. Then the taxi driver was interrupting them, asking which house.

"Right here."

Paul got out and opened the door for Clare. She picked up his jacket and handed it to him. Suddenly she felt sober.

"I'm not coming in."

"What?"

"Hold on a second," she said to the taxi driver, and got out of the car.

"What is this?" Paul asked. "The champagne in the fridge? I wasn't... I'm not taking you for granted, Clare. I put it there just in case ... in case."

Clare kissed him tenderly on the lips.

"I know. It's not you. It's me. I've had too much to drink and I don't want to do something I might regret in the morning. This has all happened a bit too fast. I'm sorry. I'll call you."

She got back into the taxi.

"Forest Fields, please."

Clare watched Paul Grace's forlorn face as the car drove away, wondering if she'd made yet another mistake or, for once, prevented herself from making one.

"This road here, duck?"

The journey had gone in a drunken flash.

"Yes, halfway up on the right."

Clare reached for her purse, looked at the meter, and groaned. She had nowhere near enough money to pay for the taxi.

21

Gary returned to uniformed duty on Monday afternoon. They'd give him a phone call Monday morning if they needed him again, DI Greasby had said. No call came.

Gary had only been with CID for a week. It felt longer. There was no warm welcome back. The greetings were less hearty than usual. You'd have thought that the long weekend would have left everyone relaxed. It seemed to have had the opposite effect.

"Ben's off sick," Jan Hunt snapped at him, "so it's a good thing you're back. I'm putting you with Clare. Walking."

"Thanks," Gary told her, sardonically.

Jan went over the information from the previous

shift. She told them the code for the day, drew their attention to offenders with curfews to observe and made sure that each officer noted down the details of vehicles stolen over the weekend. When she'd finished, she looked around for the inspector, but Paul Grace hadn't shown up yet.

"Off you go, then," Jan said.

He noticed her give Clare a funny look as they left.

Gary liked Clare. He'd rather be with her than Ben Shipman, who was a nice enough bloke, but so wound up all the time. Not a lot of humour there. Clare was warm, earthy. Gary wasn't sure, however, that she belonged in the police force. For a start, Clare looked out of place in the uniform. Her body seemed to be stuffed into it, losing all shape. Having her hair pushed back didn't suit her, either. It was only when she'd come to see him at the YMCA, the Sunday before last, wearing jeans and a cotton singlet, that he'd understood her appeal. He saw the other residents eyeing her up, understood why most male officers talked about Clare the way they did when she wasn't around, even the married ones.

"How did it go, then?" he asked, as they walked through Hyson Green.

"I'd rather not talk about it," Clare said, edgily. "The whole thing's awkward. I shouldn't have told you in the first place. I shouldn't have gone."

They walked without talking for the next ten

minutes. A few people said "Hello". A couple of shopkeepers smiled at them. There were no crimes. At Ryton, during training, they'd been told that the chance of a beat officer stumbling on a crime in progress was once every forty years, something like that. Walking the beat was a bit of a come-down from a murder investigation.

"So he wasn't gay, then?" Gary commented, as they reached the edge of their beat, the Forest.

"What makes you say that?" Clare asked, loosening up a little.

"I tried to warn you."

"You did," Clare admitted. "But I'd still like to know how you knew."

Gary thought about it. Dylan knew. Greasby knew. And he didn't even like either of them. Clare he liked. He'd rather she heard it from him than somebody else.

"Takes one to know one," he said. "Or not, in this case."

"You're..."

"Queer as they come," Gary admitted.

Clare froze, not knowing how to deal with his revelation. She knew a couple of gay people slightly but no one had ever come out to her before.

"I thought we weren't meant to use the word 'queer'," she complained.

"'Queer' is a word gays can use but straights can't," Gary told her. "It's like 'nigger'. Blacks can

use it as slang, but if whites use it, they're racists.
Are you with me?"

"I'm with you," Clare said.

She was smiling at him now. Gary decided to tell
her the rest.

"Can you keep a secret?" he asked.

"Looks like I already am doing."

She had perked up now. He had taken her mind
off her own troubles. That was something. He told
her his other secret.

"I'm the policeman who Scott Travis was trying
to blackmail."

Ruth finished work at two, went home, had a bath,
then made herself a cup of instant coffee, all the
time trying to get her courage up. Finally, she
looked in the phone book. Charlene Harris wasn't
in it, probably because she had only recently moved
to the city. Ruth tried Directory Enquiries, who told
her that the number was ex-directory. There was no
choice: Ruth rang the number she'd twice got by
dialling call return on Ben's phone. She needed to
confirm that it was Charlene's. She dialled 141
before the number. Doing that made her own call
impossible to trace.

The phone rang four times, then an answering
machine picked it up.

"I'm not home right now. Please leave a message,
and I'll get back to you as soon as I can."

Ruth recognized the silky, slightly stuck-up voice of Charlene Harris, and hung up. *Why?* she wanted to know. Why was Ben being so loving with her at the moment when, at the same time, he was still seeing Charlene? Ruth didn't understand it. There were only three options which Ruth could think of now: ignore it; confront Ben; or confront Charlene. The first two she'd tried already. They hadn't worked. Was she brave enough to try the third?

"There's no gay scene worth speaking of in Worksop, so, before I joined the police, I used to come to Nottingham on Friday, Saturday nights. I met Scott at a club once, danced with him. He was with Karen Cole. When Karen approached us the other day, I recognized her, but she didn't know me. She's still not sure where she saw me before. Nothing happened between Scott and me, but *he knew what I was*. When he saw me on the beat with Ben in Hyson Green, he knew who I was. Then he saw me in town one day. He came back to the YMCA with me."

Clare gave an involuntary gasp.

"We didn't do anything," Gary insisted. "Except that – I realize now – he tried to blackmail me. It was really awkward. He said something about how I wouldn't want people in the job to find out. I agreed that, no, I wouldn't, not at first, anyway. Then he asked to borrow some money. I told him no – you lost friends that way. When he was leaving, he asked for some money again. I offered to buy him a meal, if he was desperate. He said he wasn't hungry, and he left."

"So you knew from the start?" Clare said. "That morning, when we were guarding the crime scene."

"No," Gary told her. "I didn't see the body. It was only later, when I saw the photograph, that I realized who he was. And I didn't see any point in telling anyone. I didn't know anything about Scott. But then, that Sunday, when you came round to see me at the Y, and told me that he was a blackmailer... You remember that I rushed off?"

"You made up some story about forgetting an appointment."

"I'm sorry about that. Thing was, I realized that, in his ham-fisted way, Scott had been trying to blackmail me. I knew that if I didn't tell CID straight away and it emerged later, it'd probably cost me my job. So I rushed over there."

"And they put you on the case."

Gary nodded.

"There's a real shortage of out gay officers in Notts. I went round the gay clubs, but didn't find out anything. Scott wasn't on the scene. I don't think that was why he got himself killed."

"So the case is stalled again," Clare said.

"Unless something new comes up. That's why they put me back on the beat."

They turned on to Forest Road West. Clare asked a few more questions about the Scott Travis case and Gary answered them. They put a warning sticker on a car with an out-of-date tax disc. They turned down Southey Street and asked a prostitute on the corner of Southey Street and Hardy Street whether she knew Scott Travis or the former Georgina Williams. She didn't.

"So," Gary said, "are you going to tell me about your night out with Inspector Grace, or do I have to beat it out of you?"

She told him.

Nurses, like beat police officers, worked an eight-hour shift system. The shift that Neil needed to interview didn't come on until ten that evening, so Neil waited in the foyer of the Queen's Medical Centre for them to arrive. He'd pulled a three to eleven this week, so he was still on duty, just. He'd spent the afternoon and early evening with Tracey, trying to pick up the pieces of the inquiry into Mr Bagley's bogus caller, getting nowhere.

CID had found out a lot about the short, sad life of Scott Travis, but they were no nearer to finding out who killed him. The revelation that Pauline Jones was Scott's mother made her less, not more likely to have killed him. Neil thought that maybe Gary and Chris hadn't pressed George enough. But if it was some kind of contract killing, chances were the police would never prove it. As for Ian Jagger: Neil couldn't take the solicitor seriously as a suspect. If Jagger had wanted to get rid of Scott, he would have found a subtler way of doing it.

So here Neil was, clutching at straws. The sister showed him on to the ward. He showed the nurses on duty there the photograph of Max Walker. The sister and one of the nurses vaguely remembered him.

"You're suggesting that he might have slipped out for an hour or two and committed a crime?" the sister asked.

"That's basically it."

"It's feasible. He could go to the shower room, get changed, dodge round the desk, pretend to be a porter. But security's pretty tight around here."

"Would there be a videotape?"

There were security cameras all over the place.

"It's possible, but you'd have to search through an awful lot of them. And when was he here?"

"Two weeks ago."

"I think they'd have been erased by now."

Neil nodded. If only they'd thought of this earlier. He interviewed the nurse.

"Max did get out of bed," he said. "I remember seeing him in his dressing gown, well after lights out."

Yes! Neil thought.

"Do you know where he'd been?"

"It was the wrong direction for the toilet. If I remember correctly, there was a smell about him. Yes, that's right. He'd come from the smoking room. I remember warning him that he wouldn't want a cigarette after his op the next day – it'd be agony."

"Can you be more specific about the time?" Neil asked.

The nurse thought for a moment.

"I'd been on for a while, so it couldn't have been much before midnight. But it couldn't have been too much later than that either, or I'd have told him off for not being asleep."

"Thanks," Neil said. "You've been a lot of help."

Max could have done it, Neil realized, as he went off duty. He could. But what chance was there of them actually proving it? He tried to think of something, anything which they hadn't followed up yet. In his mind, he played back the evening he'd spent with Max, at that professor's house. The conversation had been so boring that he recalled little of it.

Neil tried to replay CID's interview with Max Walker. Looking back, it confirmed what Georgina Drew and Pauline Jones had later told them, that Scott was an incompetent blackmailer. No, wait, there was one thing which Scott had done which, now Neil thought about it, was out of character. He'd told Max that he knew who his tutor was, that he would tell him. That suggested research.

Tracking down someone's personal tutor was a bit more complicated than finding out the name of their husband. Scott had been to Max's room, though. He had probably seen the tutor's name on a folder, something like that.

But suppose Max was guilty. Suppose he'd made a slip by mentioning Scott's threat? Could Scott have approached Tim Dodd after Max refused to pay him? It made sense: Scott would be getting revenge for the beating up. Maybe Dodd rang Max, told him what Scott had said. He would have warned him about the danger of being thrown off the course if he was caught. Or maybe the professor did nothing. Loads of students used drugs of one kind or another. It wasn't a big deal.

But if that was what happened, why, when Scott got killed, didn't Professor Dodd report the conversation to the police? He wasn't to know that Max had a good alibi. There could be lots of reasons for that. Maybe, like Pauline Jones, Tim Dodd didn't read the local papers.

It was a long shot, but it was worth a try. Neil resolved to visit Professor Dodd the next day.

Clare and Gary sat in the Peacock, mulling over their third drink as last orders was called.

"I'm missing the final bus."

"I'll walk you home," Gary offered.

"Then you'll be locked out. I thought you told

me that the YMCA closed at midnight?"

"There's always someone on duty who can let you in," Gary told her. "They're used to me showing up at odd times. When I come off a night shift and go straight back to the Y, it's an hour before it's meant to be open. Makes me feel guilty, though, because I know I'm probably waking someone up. Sometimes I go to a café for an hour, unwind there."

"And tonight?" Clare asked, solicitously.

"Tonight I'm not tired. It seems a bit daft, finishing work at ten, going to bed at twelve."

"I know what you mean," Clare said. "Walk me home then. There's a spare bedroom at the moment. You can stay the night if you like."

"Thanks," Gary said. "Maybe I'll do that."

They walked up Mansfield Road, past its endless restaurants and takeaways, then down beside the graveyard where Clare had once been chased and nearly attacked. Since Clare was with Gary, they cut across the Forest, something she'd never do at this time of night if she was on her own. They were completely alone now, except for the ghosts which Clare imagined roaming the trees behind them.

"What should I do?" Clare asked Gary. "I mean, about the inspector?"

"That depends," Gary told her. "How much do you like him?"

"I hardly know him. There might be a really nice

person there. Or there could be an unscrupulous user who got me drunk because he wanted another notch on his bedpost."

"You've had blokes like that before?"

"Haven't you?"

Gary said, "Not half," and they both laughed.

"Thing is," Gary told her, "unless you get to know him better, you'll never find out, will you?"

"I guess not."

"And you did promise to ring him."

"I guess he might be hurt that I haven't."

"Well, what have you got to lose?"

"I promised myself that I'd never go out with another policeman," she told him. "Never."

"Promises to yourself are easy to break," Gary told her. "It's the ones you make to other people that you have to stand by."

He was right, Clare realized. She ought to give the inspector a chance. She couldn't let the fact that he was her boss stop that, could she? And there was something else, too: the way she'd felt in the car that night had been pretty special. Even if she blamed it on the wine and champagne, she knew that Neil had never made her feel so good. She wanted to feel that way again.

22

First thing the next morning, Neil drove to West Bridgford. He hadn't seen the Dodds' street in daylight before. It was on a wide, tree-lined road of detached houses and saloon cars, snaking up a steep hill. This was the kind of place where Neil would like to live some day, if he could afford it.

"Are you after the Dodds?" The voice's owner was concealed by bushes.

"That's right," Neil told the next-door neighbour.

"They're on holiday. Due back sometime today."

"Thanks," he told her, then thought of something. "Do you know how long they've been gone for?"

"A fortnight."

"I see. Cheers."

The Dodds had been away since Scott Travis was murdered. That could explain why Professor Dodd hadn't called the police if he had had a visit from Scott. Neil put a note through the door, asking the professor to call him at CID. He wondered if Tim Dodd would remember who he was. Not that it mattered.

Neil wasn't on duty until three in the afternoon. He would call back later, with Tracey, if the boss would allow them the time. Meanwhile, he had five hours to kill. He decided to go home and do some work on smartening up the spare room. Melanie still hadn't got anywhere to live next term. They hadn't discussed it, yet, when Mel was in Nottingham, the two of them spent most of their spare time together anyhow. If Neil made the room nice enough, maybe she'd be tempted to move in with him. It was dangerous to rush things, he knew, and her parents probably wouldn't approve, but the idea was very, very tempting...

Ruth slept badly. Yesterday, she hadn't been able to summon up the courage to go and visit Charlene, challenge her. It played on her mind all night. Then the morning started funnily. She was still on earlies. She'd got up at five, gone for a shower, realized that she'd run out of shampoo. So she'd gone into her old room, where her sports bag still was. She kept a spare bottle in it, to use after playing badminton.

Her old room wasn't empty. A bloke was asleep in the bed. Quite a nice-looking bloke, actually, with red hair and lots of muscle. Luckily, he didn't stir. He wasn't the inspector who Clare had been out with on Saturday, but he looked vaguely familiar. Clare must have copped off with him the night before. That was why she'd come home late. Ruth was kind of pleased. It was about time her friend found somebody new.

Now Ruth was coming to the end of her shift. She wondered if Ben was better. Her boyfriend had been off work ill yesterday: a stomach bug. She'd gone round to minister to his needs. If Ben was going to have today off, too, she would go straight over there after work.

"Mind if we go up this way?" she asked Mike, as they passed the bottom of Ebers Road. "I need to make a quick call."

A car which Ruth recognized was parked directly outside Ben's house. It belonged to Charlene Harris.

"I've changed my mind," Ruth told her partner. "I'll do it after work." Yet before they could turn away, Ruth saw Charlene coming out of the house, accompanied by Ben. What was going on was obvious, even to a trusting fool like her. They'd had a lunchtime quickie and now Charlene was giving Ben a lift to work. It made Ruth sick to the stomach.

The couple drove straight past Ruth and Mike, talking so intently that neither of them even noticed her.

Neil was about to set off for work when he got a message on his pager to call Ben Shipman.

"I just had Charlene round my place," Ben told him.

"I don't want to hear the details of your sex life," Neil told him.

"Give it a rest, would you? I'd really like to get Charlene off my back. I just wanted you to know that she's drawn a blank with Jagger. She talked to some people who know him. Seems the guy was heartbroken after his wife's death. No question of it not being an accident. Charlene reckons that the reason Jagger knew Scott Travis was a blackmailer is that one of Scott's victims came to him for advice. But there's no way she can find out who."

"All right," Neil said. "Thanks for your help, mate."

"Drink this week?"

"Can't. I'm on duty until eleven. I'll give you a bell at the weekend."

In the CID office, DI Greasby agreed that Neil and Tracey should visit Tim Dodd.

"But I don't buy Max Walker as a suspect. Not the type."

"What if he was on drugs?" Tracey suggested. "PCP? Angel Dust? Some kind of powerful amphetamine?"

"You're forgetting," Greasby told her, "that he'd have had to get out of a hospital bed, take the stuff, kill Scott Travis, change his clothes, sneak back into the hospital, then have an operation the next day. If he was stoned out of his mind, I think that one of the doctors or nurses might have noticed, don't you?"

Despite these arguments, Neil and Tracey drove over to the Dodds' house. They had nowhere else to go.

"You know what I think?" Tracey said.

"What *do* you think?"

"I think we've less chance of finding Scott Travis's killer than we have of finding Mr Bagley's bogus caller."

"That bad, huh?"

They pulled up outside the Dodds' detached house. A car with a GB sticker was parked in the drive.

"You say you've been to dinner here?"

"With Melanie, once."

"Think they'll remember you?"

"I guess."

"You can do the talking, then."

A tired-looking Elise Dodd answered the door. The hall was scattered with luggage and cases of wine.

"Neil! Come in. We've just got back from the Dordogne."

"Good trip?"

"Very nice, thank you. I found your note. What did you want Tim for?"

"An inquiry about one of his students who might be mixed up in a crime."

"I see. Has he called you yet?"

"Isn't he here?"

"No," Elise told them. "He went out almost as soon as we got back. Something urgent at the university, he said. Must have been important for him to hurry over there. We were driving all night. Hardly got any sleep. Shall I ask him to give you a ring when he gets in?"

"Yes, please," Neil said. "We'll let you finish unpacking."

They were at the door when Tracey thought of something. She reached into her pocket and turned back to Elise Dodd.

"I don't suppose you recognize the young man in this photo?"

Elise Dodd took the photograph of Scott Travis from her. Her tired face became paler.

"He looks like someone I used to know," she said, distractedly. "May I ask his name?"

"Scott Travis."

She nodded.

"What's Scott done?"

Neil and Tracey looked at each other. They hadn't been expecting this.

"You *know* Scott?" Neil asked.

"Yes. Excuse me. Do you mind if I sit down? I'm very tired."

"Of course," Tracey said. "I'll get you a drink."

Between sips of water, Elise Dodd told them how she came to know Scott Travis.

"Richard and I can't have children. At first, we kept trying, went to consultants, tried a range of treatments. Then we accepted it, and tried to adopt. But we were getting too old – they have a cut-off at thirty-five, can you believe that? And babies were scarce. Someone suggested fostering, and we applied.

"I wanted a little girl, but so did everybody else, it seemed. We took in Scott when he was nine. If things worked out, we thought we might adopt him. He'd had a terrible life. But we'd underestimated the size of the job we'd taken on. Scott was very hard work. He was awful at school. At home, he stole things, wet the bed, wouldn't do anything he was told to. He hated Tim. One day he took a pile of Tim's students' essays, put them on the fire. He told Tim that he cared more about the students than he did about him.

"The last straw was something that happened with next-door's little girl, while she was in the house. We never got the full story – she was too upset to tell, but it was sexual. That was when we called social services and they took him back. After Scott, understandably, we gave up on fostering. It's a great sadness in our lives. Both of us love children."

"How long was Scott with you?" Tracey asked.

"Less than six months. We moved house shortly afterwards, partly because of what had happened with Scott. It was a relief to get out of Weston Avenue, I can tell you."

"Where did you say?" Neil asked.

"Weston Avenue. It's by the Forest. Not a great area, but the house was very close to Richard's work. It was all we could afford at the time."

"What number?"

She told them. It was the house outside which Scott Travis's body had been found.

23

It was better, Ruth decided, to do it in person. She wasn't a coward. She had considered confronting Ben again, but that hadn't worked three months ago. Why should it work now? She had to face Charlene before she stole Ben back from her.

Charlene's car was outside her flat in the Park. After work, Ruth had gone round to Ben's flat, used the key he'd given her, and looked in his personal organizer. Charlene's address was in there, under "H", along with the phone number which Ruth now knew by heart. Ruth had been driving around the Park for the last hour, waiting for the lawyer to come home. She wanted to catch Charlene off her guard.

Taking a deep breath, Ruth rang the door bell.

She heard footsteps, then there was a pause. Charlene was looking through the fish eye in the door.

"Who is it?" her voice called.

"You know who I am," Ruth said, in a loud, policewoman's voice. "You know why I'm here, too."

Charlene opened the door.

"Why didn't we look in the house before?" Greasby asked.

"I checked to see if it had been broken into," Dylan explained. "It hadn't. We had a good look through the windows and the front garden was examined thoroughly, but there was no sign of any crime connected to the premises. How were we to know that Scott Travis once lived there?"

"Social services files."

"You know how useless they are. I've put in three requests for whatever records they've got on Scott Travis. No response."

"So what are we saying?" Neil asked. "Could Scott have kept a key to the house for all those years?"

"Doesn't make sense," Dylan said. "If he could get in there, why would he be squatting on Birkin Avenue? The old Dodd house is much bigger."

"Maybe it had bad memories for him," Neil suggested. "How long has Weston Avenue been empty?"

Dylan checked his notes.

"The owners are working abroad, that's why they rent it out. The previous tenants left in January. I just rang the letting agency. They did their last check on the place at the beginning of July. No one's been shown round since."

"Have they any objections to us looking over the place, or do we need a search warrant?"

"Someone from the agency's on their way over now, boss."

"Let's go, then."

Neil joined them in Dylan's car. At last, he'd discovered something useful on his own initiative. Even so, he remained pessimistic. They were unlikely to find anything in the house. But it was too big a coincidence not to investigate, Scott's body being found outside a house where he used to live.

Charlene's flat was decorated in cool white and so uncluttered that it was almost empty. The place looked like a picture from a magazine or the Habitat catalogue. Ruth couldn't imagine actually living in it.

"I suppose you'd better sit down."

Charlene didn't offer Ruth a drink. A bag was still around her shoulders. She had just come in from work.

"What do you want?" this tall, elegant woman asked.

"I want you to take my boyfriend or leave him alone," Ruth spat out. "I'm not sharing him with you."

Charlene raised both eyebrows. The whites of her eyes were like fine bone china. She scared Ruth.

"You should be talking to Ben, not me," she said.

"I've talked to Ben," Ruth told her. "I know what he says he wants. But we both know that he's weak. He finds it hard to say 'no'. Especially to you."

There was a long silence.

"You're right," Charlene finally replied. "I was always the strong one in our relationship. And now you're the strong one. I can see that."

Ruth said nothing. Charlene pulled out a chair and sat down opposite her. Then she spoke again.

"But I could never make Ben do anything he didn't want to. The police. I was against that. I tried to stop him seeing you. He wouldn't. Equally, I can't stop him seeing me."

"You're the one who does the calling," Ruth said, hoping that it was true. "Not him."

Charlene didn't argue.

"I love him," Ruth continued. "And he loves me. But he has unresolved feelings for you. I've always known that. If you really want him, you'll get him in the long run. I know that too."

"Do you?" Charlene said. "How?"

"Because you're better-looking than me. Because you're black. You're cleverer than I am, more educated, you've got more money ... but I love him and I won't share him. If you're not going to back out, then I'll have to. That's why I came to talk to you, woman to woman."

Charlene's face was cold. Ruth had no idea what she was thinking. The lawyer stood up.

"You're right," she said, "I was trying to get him back. But we haven't started up again. The only reason I've been calling him a lot recently was about a case. If you want to know, I went round to his flat this lunchtime, told him I'd found out all I could."

"Is that all?" Ruth asked. "Nothing else happened?"

Without replying, Charlene walked to the door.

"I won't call him," she said. "You can have him. I've already humiliated myself too much for Ben Shipman. Now I'd like you to leave."

In the hallway, Charlene paused before opening the front door.

"I had plans," she said, "for Ben and me. Kids, a house, a garden, the works. I expect you've got the same plans."

Ruth said nothing. Charlene continued, her voice taking on emotion.

"Let me give you a warning. What he did to me, he'll do to you. Not this week, or next week, but one day. I see it all the time in my job. Once men discover how easy it is to walk away, they do it again, and again."

"I hope not," Ruth said.

"You're the one who said it. *He's weak*. Most men are. How old are you?"

"I'll be twenty-one in a couple of weeks."

"You've still got plenty of time then. Good luck."

"Same to you," Ruth said, walking through the open door.

She got into her car and drove away, not sure whether to feel angry or relieved.

24

Tracey Wicks was working the end of Weston Avenue, just as she had been that night fifteen days before when Scott Travis was murdered.

"Found him who done it yet?" she asked.

The DI shook his head. The letting agent was waiting by the gate.

"Been inside?" Greasby enquired, as he showed him the search warrant.

"I thought it best not."

"Good. Let's go then."

It was a warm day, but, once they were through the front door, the house felt cold. The letting agent kicked aside the mail and free newspapers which obstructed the hallway.

"You two take downstairs," Greasby said to Neil and Dylan. "I'll have a look upstairs."

While the letting agent waited in the hall, Neil and the sergeant walked from room to room, opening curtains, looking in corners, wondering what the significance of the house was. The Dodds had lived there once, long ago. Scott Travis had been here for a few months. Why had he come back?

The place had been rented out for the last three years. Therefore it bore little sign of an owner's personality. The three-piece suite in the lounge looked lumpy and worn. No books were on the shelves. When Neil switched the light on, it became clear that the place needed more than a touch of paint. The window frames looked rotten. A musty smell lingered in the air.

The kitchen was the room they went into last.

"Stop!" Dylan said. "Don't put your foot in it."

Neil looked down. There was a small patch of blood in the corner, by the bin. Dylan crouched, and examined the floor.

"Someone's cleaned this," he said. "Recently. But they've missed a bit. We ought to find the mop, or whatever he's used."

"You think…"

"This could be where it happened, yeah. Don't touch anything. I'm going to get the boss."

Neil stood in the kitchen where Scott Travis might have been murdered, looking around. Hard to believe that Scott used to live here, in this big house. He had his meals cooked for him in this kitchen, and passed through that serving hatch. There was a cupboard above the fridge which hadn't been closed properly. Neil stared up at it.

Dylan had told him to touch nothing in the kitchen, and Neil didn't, not with his fingers. As Greasby was coming downstairs, he pushed the cupboard door further open with his truncheon and saw a reflection. Something had been wedged inside the cupboard, carefully positioned with a combination of cardboard and Blu-tack.

"What are you doing?" Greasby called out in an irritated voice.

"I've found something, sir. Want me to get it out or leave it where it is?"

"What have you got?" Dylan asked, impatiently.

Gently, Neil pushed the door fully open, revealing the object concealed inside it.

"Scott Travis's video camera," he said.

25

The video's opening minutes showed an empty kitchen with fluorescent lighting. One of the work surface drawers was pulled half open. There was no sound to begin with. Then there was a knock on the door. Scott Travis, as alive as the last time Gary saw him, walked across the kitchen and opened it.

"Hi, Tim," Scott said to the fortyish man who stood in the doorway, looking anxiously about him. "Come in."

"What's going on?" the professor asked, stepping inside. "Why are you here?"

"I had to get you to come round the back so that no one saw," Scott explained, his voice wobbly with nervousness. "This house is meant to be empty."

"You kept a key?"

Scott smiled, a weak, pathetic smile.

"In case I wanted to come back, yeah. I never used it, though. Not till tonight."

Tim Dodd shuffled his feet and looked around.

"I haven't got long," he said. "Elise and I are going on holiday in the morning. You said it was a matter of life and death."

"That depends, doesn't it?" Scott said.

"What do you mean?" the professor demanded.

"Depends whether you want Elise finding out what you used to do to me."

The professor's eyes narrowed. "I don't know what you're talking about," he said.

Scott's voice became high-pitched, barely in control.

"Yes, you do. In my bedroom, after she'd gone to bed. You'd come in, wake me up and do it to me. Every night. Three months. You told me you'd kill me if I told anyone. Kill me."

On camera, the two men stared at each other. Scott was trembling. Tim Dodd was trembling too. The professor's eyes burned with anger and contempt, but his voice betrayed what was going on in his mind.

"There's this thing," Tim Dodd said, fear making him high-pitched. "False memory syndrome. That's what you must be suffering from, Scott. I'm sorry for you. I expect you need some money. I'll give you some. But you mustn't repeat accusations like that. They'd lock you away."

Scott's voice became a hysterical whine.

"I'll repeat them to who I like. There's no time limit on child abuse, you know. Ten years is nothing."

"You don't have any proof," Dodd said. "It'd be my word against yours." Scott was ready for this.

"But mud sticks, dunnit? When I tell Elise, she'll put things together. Times when she woke up in the night and you weren't there. Those fresh sheets that appeared on the bed in the morning. She'll work it out."

Tim Dodd clenched his fist. Gary saw him looking at the open kitchen drawer. His voice became that of a snake.

"If you tell Elise, I'll do what I threatened back then, Scott. I'll kill you. You've got no proof of anything you say, Scott. You're worthless. You were worthless then and you're nothing now, do you hear me? Now, I'm going to give you some money, and then I never want to see you again."

Dodd reached for his wallet, but Scott had lost interest in the money.

"How many others did you do it to, eh? That little girl next door. You blamed that on me, didn't you? How many others, eh?"

"You've got no proof," Dodd said. "Take the money and go."

"No proof?" Scott screamed. "You've more or less admitted it! And I've got a tape recorder in my pocket. So I want..."

But he didn't get to finish the sentence. Tim Dodd reached into the half-open kitchen drawer and took out a rolling pin. It could, Neil guessed, as easily have been a knife. The professor had gone over the edge. He began to beat Scott with the blunt block of wood. Dodd bashed the boy's head and chest, knocking him to the floor, out of sight of the camera lens. They could hear Scott whimpering.

"Now give me the tape," Dodd said.

"I lied," Scott groaned. "There isn't a tape."

Dodd laughed, a horrible manic laugh.

"You always were a stupid boy," he said.

The rest of the beating took place off camera. When it was over, Dodd left the room. He returned with a sheet of clear plastic, which he wrapped Scott's body in. Then he set about cleaning the kitchen floor. He was still at it when the camcorder battery ran out.

The three CID officers drove to West Bridgford. None of them spoke. It was one thing to know that someone had been beaten to death, another to see it happening before your eyes. After watching the video, before getting into the car, Neil had gone to the gents, where he was sick. The thought that he had eaten dinner with Dodd, that Melanie had been in his house, and in his office … it made him want to be sick again.

Scott Travis was a drug dealer and a blackmailer, Neil knew, but an incompetent and pathetic one. You couldn't blame him for what he had become. Abandoned by his mother, raped by his foster father, his life had been thrown into the rubbish bin before he was ten years old. What chance did he ever have of leaving a life of crime, of finding a job, of finding love?

"Car's not there," Neil told the others as they pulled up outside the house. "It looks like he isn't back yet."

"You'd better do the talking," Greasby told Neil. "No point in letting the wife know what's going on until we've got the bastard in custody."

Elise Dodd answered the door. She had washed her hair and changed into a dress, but there were still lines of tiredness, or anxiety, around her eyes.

"Hasn't Tim contacted you yet?"

Neil shook his head.

"Where is he?"

"He rang up and I told him you'd been round. He said he'd call you from his solicitor's. That's where he is now – one of his students is in some trouble, he said."

"Can you tell me who his solicitors are?" Neil asked.

"Jagger and Co. They're…"

"I know where they are. Thanks."

"Can't you tell me what's…"

But Neil was already getting back into the car.

It was a hot, late afternoon as they drove into Nottingham, past the cricket ground, over Trent Bridge, round the back of the Broadmarsh Centre and into the city itself. The traffic on Maid Marian Way was starting to thin. Loud young men in shirt sleeves were drinking outside the Castle gates. Uniformed security guards were stopping cars without resident's passes from entering the Park. A pale red sun lingered above the old city hospital like a faded bloodstain.

Ian Jagger was locking up his offices as they pulled up outside the solicitor's. Greasby jumped out of the car.

"We're looking for one of your clients, Professor Dodd."

The solicitor pointed at his vintage Jaguar.

"He's in there. I was just about to bring him over to you. My client has a confession to make."

"That he murdered Scott Travis?"

Jagger pursed his lips.

"He's hoping the charge will be manslaughter."

Without the videotape, it probably would have been. Greasby didn't hide the disgust on his face.

"He hasn't a hope in hell," the inspector told the solicitor.

Just like Scott Travis, Neil thought.

EPILOGUE

As soon as she got off the phone with Ben, Charlene stormed round to her boss's place, getting there just as the solicitor's SV12 pulled up outside.

"Charlene!" he said with a broad, if tired, smile. "I've only just finished work. What a pleasant surprise after a tiresome day. Come in, come in."

But Charlene wasn't having any of his old-world charm.

"You used me!" she shouted as soon as they were inside his house. "You wanted me to find out that Travis was a blackmailer and tell Ben."

"I did," Jagger admitted, pouring himself a stiff drink. "My contacts told me that the police had no inkling that Travis was a blackmailer. I wanted to help – them and you."

He held up the decanter to offer Charlene a drink. She shook her head.

"Why?" she asked.

Jagger gave her a sad smile.

"I owed you a favour, Charlene. You see, I *did* use you three months ago, over the arson case. The information I gave you was accurate, that's how I justified it to myself. But it was also misleading. By letting Phoenix stay free to commit more arson, I could have cost you your life. That was unforgivable. I apologize, sincerely. It will never happen again. Will you accept my apology?"

Charlene wasn't so easily placated. "Only when you've finished the explanation. Why get to the police through me?"

"Because it would put you in the good books of your policeman friend. I'm not blind, Charlene. It's obvious how much you care for him."

"Used to."

Jagger ignored this comment.

"I feel – in some ways – responsible for your breakup. I could have got the information to the police by another means, probably, but I thought that this way would bring the two of you closer together. Was I wrong?"

"Not entirely," Charlene said, trying to hold on to her anger. "Anyway, what about client/lawyer privilege? Tim Dodd was your client. Presumably he came to you for advice, about what to do when he was being blackmailed?"

"Yes. He came for my advice before going to see Scott and the advice I gave him remains confidential. I certainly didn't tell him to kill the boy."

"Did you know he did it?" she asked.

"Not for sure. But I knew of his potential for violence. There was an incident a few years ago. That was when he first became my client. The case never came to court. I helped him to keep it quiet. Even his wife didn't know."

"You breached professional ethics," Charlene accused him.

"I did not," Jagger asserted. "There is only one set of circumstances where disclosure is appropriate. I gave you the strongest hint, by talking about the Children Act. Scott Travis was only nine years old when Dodd abused him. You could argue that Scott is dead and could not be endangered, but there might be other children at risk. I have nothing to reproach myself for."

"No," Charlene said. "I can see that you don't."

"So, do you accept my apology?"

"I do," she said, with all the dignity she could muster.

"Perhaps you'd let me seal the apology by taking you out to dinner tomorrow?"

"You've bought me two meals now," Charlene told him. "Let me treat you."

Jagger didn't need to weigh up the idea for more than two seconds.

"Invitation accepted."

The phone rang and the solicitor answered it.

"Elise? Have you see him? No. Of course I understand. You must be very concerned. Better that I explain in person. Give me ten minutes."

He put down the phone and sighed.

"I'm sorry, Charlene. I have to leave you. It seems that my client is too ... emotional to talk to his wife. She has no idea what's happened."

"What are you going to tell her?" Charlene asked.

"I wish I knew," the lawyer muttered. "But I'll think of something. I always do."

Gary and Clare were summoned to see Paul Grace towards the end of their shift. The inspector was the last person who Clare wanted to see. She still hadn't worked up the nerve to talk to him. All week, they had been avoiding each other.

"Seems CID have a videotape of Scott Travis being murdered," Grace told the two of them. "I've had DI Greasby on the phone, commending both of you for your help with this case."

"Who was it, sir?" Clare asked.

The inspector told them.

"Dodd meant to dump Scott Travis in the Trent," he ended, "but when he'd dragged the body out of the house there were two prostitutes at the end of Weston Avenue and he was scared that one of them might see him loading the car. So he dropped the body just inside the gate, went home and washed the plastic sheeting, binned his bloody clothes, then set off on holiday the following morning. When he got back a fortnight later and found that Neil had called to see him, he assumed he'd been rumbled and went straight to his solicitor, Ian Jagger. Jagger advised him to give himself up."

"Why give himself up?" Clare asked. "If Dodd didn't know there was any evidence?"

Grace shrugged.

"You'd have to ask Mr Jagger."

"Would it be all right if we went over there, sir? I'd like to know…"

"Fine. Go now if you like. Gary, would you check in those radios? I need a quiet word with Clare."

"Sir."

Outmanoeuvred, Clare avoided the inspector's eyes. When they were alone, he coughed. Paul Grace looked as nervous as Clare felt. He spoke very quietly.

"I just wanted to say, Clare, if it would make life easier, we'll pretend that Saturday night never happened. I feel bad about it. I'm your senior officer and I asked a favour of you. I was … exploiting my situation and it was wrong of me to conceal my true feelings. But then I had a few drinks and got carried away."

"Me, too," Clare said.

"So what do you say?" The inspector asked.

Clare stared at the floor. She was twenty years old, but she had never felt more like a teenager.

"This is awkward," she said.

"We can pretend…"

"No," Clare told him, "pretending's no good. I felt something. I can't act as though I didn't. But it's complicated, and I don't know how I feel now. I don't know how I feel about anything. Last month, I finished with someone who kept telling me that I was the love of his life. Two weeks later, he'd found someone new and she's practically moved in with him. Do you know what that did to my self esteem?"

"I can have a good guess," Paul said.

"And now you… Oh, I don't know. Half the time I think I want to see you again and half the time I want to change shifts."

"Don't do anything drastic," Paul pleaded.

"I don't know what to do," Clare said, wishing that she was anywhere but here.

"Why don't we take things very, very slowly?" Paul Grace suggested.

Clare looked at him. His eyes were kind, thoughtful.

"OK," she said.

"I'm only interested in an equal relationship," Paul told her. "When you're ready, maybe you could ask me out. How about that?"

Clare smiled.

"What are you doing Saturday night?" she asked.